I0730001

EDITED BY

Paula Dias Garcia,
Sam Agar,
Marc Clohessy &
Aran Kelly

Sans.
PRESS

LIMERICK

2025

OUT
THERE

OUT THERE

ISBN: 978-1-7384962-1-1
Published by Sans. PRESS
September 2025
Limerick, Republic of Ireland

COVER ARTWORK by Andreea Dumuta
ILLUSTRATIONS by Julie de Graag
LAYOUT & BOOK DESIGN by Paula Dias Garcia
TYPESET in Bembo MT Pro and Espiritu

EDITORS
Paula Dias Garcia, Sam Agar,
Marc Clohessy & Aran Kelly

www.sanspress.com
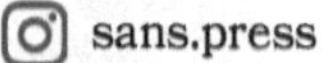
@PressSans
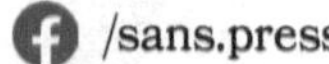
sans.press
/sans.press

Collection © Sans. PRESS, 2025
Individual contributions © individual authors, 2025
Cover artwork © 2024 by Andreea Dumuta
Reprinted with permission of the illustrator.
All authors and artists retain the rights to their own work.

OUT THERE gratefully receives
financial assistance from the Arts Council.

PAULA DIAS GARCIA

EDITOR'S NOTE

If you, like ourselves, have made speculative fiction your bread & butter, at some point you have thrust a manuscript at an unsuspecting relative to hear back a very non-committal, '...it's a bit out there, isn't it?'

And, in fairness to them, it probably is. There are aliens and fairies, spaceships and ancient curses. There's probably some body horror – *of course* there's body horror. If you go to our very core of humanity, to the nervous centre of our vulnerability, what you'll find is usually a horrible, horrible mess.

What we keep asking of you, though, and of our often frightened relatives, is to bear with us. Because the question we keep trying to answer with our weird stories is still the same – how else would we talk about reality? How would you go about talking about an indescribable loss if not with aliens, or a cursed forest dweller? How to talk about the weight of family without curses, or that of relationships without gore? Is there really a way to talk about nostalgia, desire and heartbreaks without any feral instinct, without ending with a mouth full of blood?

In the strange ways of bibliomancy, I was introduced to a Barry Taylor quote by way of John Green; in talking about his theological beliefs, he quotes that "God is the name of the blanket we throw over mystery to give it shape." In a similar way, fiction is the blanket we have found to throw over that which is too large for us all to hold otherwise, too formless to speak about without some manufactured boundary.

So please, bear with us. Don't let the strangeness of the frame keep you from the picture – yes, even if it is oozing something that looks suspiciously like blood. There will be bones, and strange offerings, love found and lost, and fairies, spaceships and witches. There will be honesty to it all.

Once again, thank you to all that have allowed us to keep chasing the mystery – to all the writers who trust us with their work, lecturers who share our calls and booksellers promoting our books; to the Arts Council and our growing community of readers.

We couldn't be prouder to share *Out There* with all of you. Trust us, this one will be weird – we don't know any other way to be real.

THE STORIES

BECAUSE I AM WRITING ANOTHER
    HORROR SCREENPLAY ⚡ *Amy Lynne Mckenzie*   11

EDEN ON THE FAR SIDE ⚡ *Frédéric Mathieu*   31

I GET ALONG WITHOUT YOU VERY WELL ⚡ *Anna Ní Dhúill*   41

BEAN SÍ ⚡ *Éadie Long*   49

PROSPERITY ⚡ *Danielle Mullen*   67

THE SKULL PAINTER ⚡ *Nora Schinnerl*   85

INFILTRATION ⚡ *Amanda M. Blake*   101

DRINKERS ⚡ *Corey Farrenkopf*   117

THE EATING MONTH ⚡ *Aisling Ní Choibheanaigh Nic Eoin*   129

MALL RAT ⚡ *Scotty Sarafian*   137

GRUB ⚡ *Kit Calvert*   147

DO NOT STARE AT THE SUN ⚡ *Ross McCleary*   159

THE UNDRY ⚡ *Paul Mulholland*   181

ENSNARED ⚡ *Máire T. Robinson*   199

DEATH OF A BEACHCOMBER ⚡ *Blaise Gilburd*   209

THE AUTHORS   217

CONTENT WARNINGS

Please be advised that discussions of death, grief and sexuality may be present throughout the book.

Injury detail: *Because I'm Writing Another Horror Screenplay, Bean Sí, Ensnared*

Death of a child: *Bean Sí*

Gore: *Because I'm Writing Another Horror Screenplay, The Skull Painter, Ensnared*

Domestic Abuse: *Because I'm Writing Another Horror Screenplay (referenced)*

Substance Abuse: *Do Not Stare at the Sun (referenced), The Undry*

Suicide: *Drinkers (referenced)*

Serious Illness: *Eden on the Far Side*

Violent Death: *Bean Sí*

Large scale death: *Do Not Stare at the Sun (referenced)*

IMAGE LIST

The images used in the interior of *Out There* are public domain prints from artist Julie de Graag, available in the online archive of the Rijksmuseum, Amsterdam.

Gift of M.J. de Graag

December, *p. 05*

Varens, *p. 11*

Rozenstruik, *p. 31*

Twee konijnen, *p. 41*

Druipende paddenstoel, *p. 49*

Geranium, *p. 67*

Memento mori, *p. 85*

Cactusbloem, *p. 101*

Zittende kat, *p. 117*

Dood vogeltje, *p. 129*

Muis, *p. 137*

Rups op een tak, *p. 147*

Zittende kat, *p. 159*

Zwaan in het water, *p. 181*

Spin in een web, *p. 199*

Schelp, *p. 209*

Drie katten, *p. 217*

THE WORMS AT HEAVEN'S GATE

Out of the tomb, we bring Badroulbadour,
Within our bellies, we her chariot.
Here is an eye. And here are, one by one,
The lashes of that eye and its white lid.
Here is the cheek on which that lid declined,
And, finger after finger, here, the hand,
The genius of that cheek. Here are the lips,
The bundle of the body and the feet.
. . . .
Out of the tomb we bring Badroulbadour.

WALLACE STEVENS

AMY LYNNE MCKENZIE

BECAUSE I AM WRITING ANOTHER HORROR SCREENPLAY

1

My husband allows me to film our bed at night.

2

The working title of my new screenplay is AT THE END OF THE DARK. The **LOGLINE** is: *After a husband and wife amicably decide to divorce, their last night together is riddled with demonic disturbances, culminating in shocking revelations.* What those shocking revelations are, I haven't yet discovered. But I am hopeful having hours of footage of myself and my husband sleeping will spur this along, provide inspiration, as I don't have much time left to finish the screenplay.

3

We attempt to power on the old Nikon my husband had (accidentally) stolen from his undergraduate cinematography class, which never morphed into a career, even with his MA in film studies; he's in real estate now, which is why I get to stay home and write screenplays we pretend will be picked up by a mythical millionaire exec. The camera battery is dead and refuses to charge. We Amazon a new one. And because I feel guilty about the exorbitant amount of purchases we ship to our doorstep, my overly large share of consumption, I also order a compost bin for our backyard.

4

My screenplay opens with the husband and the wife casually discussing pros and cons of separation. They drink French-press coffee at the breakfast table. They smile. They care for the other's wellbeing. They are more than civil; but the love is over, the love is dead. No amount of wailing, no amount of roping the moon will resuscitate it. They model decency in silky pyjama sets, nibbling petite slices of organic cantaloupe from the farmer's market on silver flashing forks. He dribbles juice on his chin and she uses a cotton napkin to pat him clean — a spark of worry on her face.

             WIFE
    But who will take care of you?
    You are helpless.

Well, that chafes him, upstanding man in silky pyjamas paying all the bills himself from his real estate sales, you can imagine. His voice rises. He blames her weird art for the divorce. But the wife politely nibbles cantaloupe like he's telling her how good a day it would be for a picnic. The camera pans: the walls are covered with giant, over-human-sized paintings of dreary demon men. A demon man smoking a cigarette alone in bed. A demon man hunched into a whisky glass at a neon-lit bar. A demon man gobbling pizza in his car. A demon man rocking a wary-eyed baby. Even a demon man with tears streaming down his cheeks as he adds the carrot nose to a grinning snowman. The husband, still berating on, and the wife, still listening attentively, avoid looking at the demons. They pretend they do not exist. I believe, if I've read *The Screenwriter's Bible* correctly, this is called the **CATALYST**.

The new battery arrives wrapped in plastic, wrapped in styrofoam, wrapped in cannot-be-recycled twist ties. We soon discover that we ordered the wrong battery. Turns out a battery for a DSLR D2H will not, in fact, work on a DSLR D810 as the charts we consulted online led us to believe. I try to return it, but *LORD*. We order another without returning the first battery, which I feel bad about – *another* battery in the landfill? I'm sure Mother Earth is applauding. And the money, only fourteen dollars and some odd cents, I worry about that wasted money. Because real estate is doomed, you know. I can feel the clock ticking, the recession pulling me away from Final Draft with its sweet automatic tabs and French-press-coffee-at-the-breakfast-table formatting, back towards my previous job as a beleaguered high school English teacher, which was enough to make anyone wish to write screenplays, even if they are always about demonic disturbances.

6

So far, the wife's best dialogue is:

<pre>
                    WIFE
         Surely it wouldn't hurt?
         One last time?
</pre>

The husband, still offended, is only further affronted. He thinks sex is no good for people on the outs. He will not allow it. But — because a wine glass slides off the kitchen counter on its own accord, because he frowns into the bathroom mirror and his reflection smiles back, because their house is wallpapered in leering demons — the husband allows himself to be talked into sleeping in the same bed with his soon-to-be-ex wife. He allows himself to be licked into a final blowjob from his soon-to-be-ex wife. *The Screenwriter's Bible* calls this **THE BIG EVENT**.

7

'Where did it come from?' my husband asks. He fiddles with the tripod, then angles the camera toward me. I lie on our bed as though in a coffin, with my arms crossed over my chest. We are still waiting for the new battery and so we are only practicing, acclimatizing ourselves to sleeping with a lens pointed at our faces: a dress rehearsal of sorts. 'What?' I ask, reanimating my corpse to answer him. 'Your obsession with horror.' '*My* obsession with horror?' He shortens a tripod leg. 'Yeah, *your* obsession with horror.' I resume corpse pose. 'It started with you,' I say. 'Trying to figure out how to survive you.' I say this cutting, like an insult. But it is a joke. We know it is a joke. It is the exact kind of joke we always make. We laugh.

8

Funny, the couple in my screenplay likes horror movies, too. They cannot remember which one of them started this insular mania, but they cannot get enough. They are ravenous. They feel there is always a gap in their horror movie knowledge, a hunger for the undiscovered. Whatever they watched last was a disappointment, fell flat on its fucking face, a dismal disgrace, it should have been better, what a shame. Whatever they watch next could be *the thing*. They are searching, they are searching, they are snobs really. Really nothing would sate them. But they don't know that. The husband and the wife's horror movie obsession is all **BACKSTORY**. I don't have it in the right place in the screenplay, and I don't know how to squeeze it in before the **CATALYST**, in the first ten pages, which is necessary according to *The Screenwriter's Bible*.

9

The 250 composting worms I ordered online arrive before the new camera battery. With the addition of a few warm days, there are suddenly millions of worms in my compost bin. My little wormies, I call them. I feed them kitchen scraps, mostly onions we let go soft and reeking banana skins and stinky take-out food we never got around to finishing. In the afternoons, I like to leave the demonic disturbances with Final Draft and dig into the steaming compost and watch the wormies wriggle from daylight. One sunny afternoon, our neighbour appears on the other side of the fence that divides us. She is very nice; she once told me she traveled to Vermont for her sister's 102nd birthday and she said this with such pride, it melted my heart. I doubt she watches horror movies and I wonder what she thinks of our costly Sonos subwoofer and sound bar, which we bought before the recession to make our horror-movie viewings scarier. I wonder what she thinks of my screaming at jump scares, which I do even when I'm not frightened simply because I like to scream. I toss the wormies their daily allowance of soft onions and I say, 'Hi! Isn't this weather dreamy?' The neighbour and I exchange normal pleasantries. She suddenly makes a funny face and I worry she smells the onions or glimpses my 346,792,928,475,953,948,679,248,659,999 worm friends, or perhaps she's noticed the mountain of Amazon boxes clogging our front door. I brace myself. 'You know,' she says carefully, clasping her bony hands together, 'your husband isn't very kind to you.' She peers into my eyes. 'I can hear him. I can help you if— ' I laugh and she startles. 'We watch a lot of horror movies,' I say. 'That's why I'm screaming all the time.' This only serves to confuse my neighbour. 'It's not like that,' I continue, more honestly. 'That's how we joke. We are sarcastic people.

And you hear him because his voice is loud. You don't hear the wild things *I* say.' This alarms her, nice woman with her nice long-living sister, you can imagine. So I exclaim, laughing to prove I'm not some delusional battered woman, 'Look at all my wormies! We are diverting our food scraps from landfills.' And our nice neighbour says, stepping back inside the safety of the fence that divides us, 'Oh. I was thinking about getting worms for my compost.' So I exclaim, graciously to prove I'm not some delusional battered woman, 'Take some of ours! We have millions!' And what can she do but accept? Her cupped hands trembling as I fill them with wormies and soft rotting onions.

10

I muse. Maybe that's what my screenplay is missing? Maybe **THE BIG EVENT** is not the errant blowjob, but actually the nice neighbour telling the wife that her husband isn't very kind; she can hear him. And the wife is puzzled by this. She can't figure out if it's true or not. He pays all the bills? They have many shared interests, such as horror movies? And though the husband provides the wife with the financial ability to pursue her art – those dreary, ugly paintings of sorrowful demons – she is not always as happy as she should be. Her feelings are shapeshifters. One minute the wife loves her wormies, the next she sees them as an excuse not to address the heart of the problem: her ravenous need to consume consume consume. To demonstrate this need, I have the wife secretly pick up an extra-large stuffed-crust meat-lovers pizza and devour it in her car, slice on top of slice, while driving home to her soon-to-be-ex husband. She tears the pizza box into tiny pieces and feeds the greasy cardboard to her worms in her backyard compost bin. She burps. Then she goes inside for dinner. At the table, her husband serves her a few sauteed asparagus spears. She dribbles them with lemon juice.

```
              WIFE
  Yum! I want to gobble this up!
             HUSBAND
             (warns)
  Go easy on the lemon. You don't
  want  to  overwhelm  the  char
  flavour.
```

The chronological placement of this scene is all wrong. So would that then make the errant blowjob the **CATALYST**? And not **THE BIG EVENT**? Can pieces of plot be swapped, exchanged, manhandled so easily? Is that cheating? *The Screenwriter's Bible* does not say.

11

My husband comes in from showing another house. 'How'd it go?' I ask. He sighs, shakes his head. I rub his shoulder consolingly. 'How's your day going?' he asks. I consider my wormies, wriggling from the light, copulating in their little wormie knots, fleshy, all secretion, all different shades of pink, all different thicknesses – thin as a hair, fat as a pencil. 'Good,' I say. 'And the screenplay?' he asks. I sigh, shake my head. 'I lost the plot.' Then I am crying, keening into my laptop. 'I'll never get it right. There is no mythical millionaire exec waiting for me. I'm average! I'm not really good at all.' My husband rubs my shoulder consolingly. 'You're right,' he says. 'You're the worst writer there ever was. Deplorable. Lousy. Derivative. And I hate you for it.' He kisses my forehead and I laugh bravely through my tears. 'We'll have the camera footage tomorrow. That will help.' 'Sure,' I say. 'What do you want for dinner?' he asks. 'We could order a stuffed-crust meat-lovers. To cheer you up?' 'Perfect.' He kisses me again before he goes off to fiddle with the camera: tonight's the big night. We got the correct battery; he's figured out the night vision. What would our nice neighbour think? She is just so wrong. If I had been my husband, watching me cry over the misplacement of another demonic disturbance, I would have beat the absolute shit out of me.

12

After the errant blowjob, the husband and wife go to bed: here comes the **MIDPOINT**. The husband turns fitfully on his side, facing the door. The wife turns fitfully on her side, facing the wall. Symbolic, I know. They try to sleep. Restlessly at first, shifting blankets and juggling pillows. Then the husband snores softly. The wife whimpers. The camera holds for so long it feels intrusive, watching people who don't know they are being watched. Suddenly, as if time jumped, the husband stands on the wife's side of the bed. He leans over her.

HUSBAND
(whispers)

Darling, darling, honeycake.
Wake up.

She frowns in her sleep – she does not want to wake. She believes this is the morning of their separation. She does not want to face this.

HUSBAND
Fire of my loins, idol of my
heart, wake up.

Well, that wakes up the wife who swallowed her husband's cum only to get his cold shoulder in return, you can imagine. She eyes him suspiciously.

WIFE
Have you been drinking?
HUSBAND
(laughs)
Come with me.

He suavely kisses her fingers and takes her by the hand; he helps her out of bed. Their eyes locked, they walk out the bedroom door. Perhaps he will go down on her now, because you have been left feeling the imbalance of their sex; like an ear infection, it makes you woozy. After a long moment, the camera pans from the empty doorway to the bed. Where the husband of the errant blowjob, of the unreturned orgasm, sleeps soundly.

13

'Are you sure?' My husband wants my consent. 'If this is done, it cannot be undone,' he says. 'Like cutting off all your hair,' I say, running my fingers over his nearly bald head. 'Like quitting your teaching job of fifteen years,' he says, elbowing me in the ribs. 'Like that blowjob,' I say. He laughs. I suavely kiss his fingers and take him by the hand. I lock my eyes on his: 'I'm sure.' My husband nods bravely. 'Me, too. Anything if it will help you get this screenplay figured out.' He presses record. We lie down in the bed, facing each other. Symbolic, I know. We think of our future selves watching us, gray green in the dark, and knowing we were thinking about them. I sit up. I smile at the camera and wave to my future self. My husband catches my waving hand. He whispers, 'You're giving me the creeps.'

14

The husband of the errant blowjob wakes to an empty bed. He throws back the covers. He hates the wife for sneaking out of bed when he's sleeping. What a nasty trick! Her roaming the empty dark house in her robe, like a ghost of female vengeance. Her footsteps on the hardwood are the sound of rebuke, reproach, reprimand. He's had enough. He rears up out of bed.

HUSBAND OF THE ERRANT BLOWJOB
Goddamn it!

He must find her, bring her back to bed, where he can keep an eye on her. Where she can't do anything stupid. He stomps down the hallway. He blusters into the kitchen. Upon the breakfast table, lit by the romantic brilliance of a hundred candles: hunks of golden cantaloupe and ruby watermelon; bloody pomegranates ripped open, leaking; split peaches and nectarines the colour of sunsets; apples, yes of course, apples! apples heaped like treasures men kill each other for; oh my god, the plums with their tart skins and the apricots with their honeyed flesh. Amid this pagan feast, the suave husband laps up the wife. She is in ecstasy; so joyous, she giggles. She rips a cherry from the stem with her teeth, swallows even the pit. Her nipples are covered in the jewels of raspberries. On her head, a crown of grapevines. Between her moaning, her whimpers of delight and pleasure and surrender:

WIFE
I want to eat it all!

HUSBAND OF THE ERRANT BLOWJOB
Louise!

The wife looks at the kitchen doorway and sees her husband in his silky pyjamas, the husband who pays all the bills from his real estate sales, the husband who her neighbour says is not so kind. The wife turns with horror to the husband between her legs. The suave husband gazes upon her. His chin shines with the succulence of mangoes, the lushness of the wife's cunt. This is the **CRISIS**.

15

My husband falls to sleep as if the camera is not watching us from its self-righteous tripod perch, the little red recording light upon our faces. But I cannot sleep, knowing in the morning I will watch this footage of me restlessly tossing, knowing I was thinking about watching my future self in the morning, knowing the footage won't help me write the screenplay in the least — it is simply a diversion. I sneak out of bed and roam the empty dark house in my robe, like a ghost of female despair. My footsteps on the hardwood are the sound of failure, defeat, ruin. I stand in our empty living room and I wonder what the walls would look like covered in giant, human-sized paintings of dreary demons. Alas, my husband is not the dickhead husband in the screenplay; he is kind, in spite of, maybe because of, our mean little jokes. It is how we comfort each other: I will verbalise your worst fear, then you will realise how silly you are being. Perhaps my supportive kind husband is *why* this screenplay will go nowhere — because my fiction is too fake. If he was truly cruel, truly the husband of the errant blowjob, I might be inspired. For consolation, I slip outside and head for my compost bin. The night is dark with the new moon and our nice neighbour waits for me. We are both barefoot. 'It's not my husband,' I explain. 'He's a kind man.' She nods slowly, her neck creaking and cracking; she is ancient, I realise. Her 102-year-old sister must be the baby of the family. She says, in a voice as old as the cold wind that blows around us, 'I was wrong. I am not often wrong. Nine times out of ten, it's men. Used to be, it was *only* men.' Our nice neighbour rolls her dull, primeval eyes. 'You women these days. With your big dreams.' I shrug, apologising on behalf of my entire generation of tricksy women. 'Tell me then, why this hunger?' our nice neighbour murmurs. 'I see it.' She swirls her long, crooked fingers through the air, as if they can taste my anguish. 'A shadow of desperation all around you. You are starving.' I try to explain, 'I lost the plot. I'll never get it right. There is no mythical millionaire exec waiting for me. I'm average. I'm not really good at all.' 'Ah,' she says. 'Ah!' Her dull eyes sparkle to life. 'You're right. You're deplorable. Lousy. Derivative. No one wants your boring stories. You were better off an old frumpy teacher – at least you were useful then.' It is a relief to hear her honesty, something other than my husband's silly faith in me. 'Can you help?' I ask. I reach for her, but she pulls back. 'It will cost you. Something dear. Something *kind*.' I've watched enough horror movies, written enough horror screenplays, to know this was coming. 'I'm willing,' I say. She smiles, clasps her bony hand with mine.

16

HUSBAND OF THE ERRANT BLOWJOB
Louise! What are you eating!

A banquet of luscious fruit does not weigh upon the breakfast table. No, no. The wife is covered in wormies. 346,792,928,475,953,948,679,248,659,999 wormies, copulating in their little wormie knots, fleshy, all secretion, all different shades of pink, all different thicknesses – thin as a hair, fat as a pencil. Wormies and soft rotting onions. She screams. She runs her hands over and over her naked body to get them off! off! off!

SUAVE HUSBAND (V.O.)
Louise.

The resonant depth of the suave husband's voice fills the house. It stops the scream in the wife's throat. She goes as still as death. The suave husband takes her face into his hands.

SUAVE HUSBAND
Look again.

The wife looks again. Her long hair is tangled with baby strawberries, delicate leaves and precious white blossoms. Beneath her feet, furry skins of kiwi, prickle of a pineapple, the miracle of figs. She gasps.

SUAVE HUSBAND (V.O.)
(sadly)
It's not the first time he's
deceived you.

The suave husband holds a bronze pear to the wife's lips. Their eyes lock. She does not hesitate: she bites in.

HUSBAND OF THE ERRANT BLOWJOB
(horrified)
Louise! You are eating worms!

The wife whirls to him. Her eyes flash. Her molars crunch.

17

My husband stands beside me in our moonless backyard. He is not in silky pyjamas but in boxer briefs and an old t-shirt from a never-heard-of indie band from a show he went to way back when he still went to shows, when he was a cinematography major, before he gave up his dreams so he could make enough money to support mine. The maple trees blow in the breeze, waving branches which always seem so rigid, but are actually elastic, dancing and working up to the big dramatic moment, like the emphatic gestures of a Greek chorus. 'What are you doing?' my husband asks. I am on my tiptoes, leaning into my compost bin, buried up to my elbows in my wormies; I do not mind the smell, which is of rot returning to the earth. And it is warm. My compost bin gives off heat. I try to explain, 'I wanted to see what they do at night.' My husband stares. I try again, 'I'm not sure if they sleep.' My husband blinks. 'The worms,' I say. My husband breathes out of his mouth. Then I finally land on the correct words, 'For my screenplay.' My husband sighs with relief, 'Of course.' I can get away with most anything if I say it is for my fictions. He peers around the dark backyard, searching. 'I thought I heard you talking to someone?' 'No.' 'Well, what's the verdict?' 'What?' I ask, startled. 'Do the worms sleep?' 'Oh.

Not that I can tell,' I say, 'but I'll need to do more research. Why don't you go back to bed? I'm going to get some writing done.' My husband frowns. 'Now? It's like three in the morning.' I smile beatifically. 'I was struck by inspiration.' He grins. 'That's wonderful.' He rubs my shoulder consolingly.

18

In revision, I **FLASHBACK** to the scene with the nice neighbour, when she tells the wife her husband isn't very kind. The nice neighbour, her hands full of wormies and soft onions, gazes upon the wife. The niceness cracks from her face like a mud mask gone dry.

NICE NEIGHBOUR

```
I can get him to be kinder. A
little more romantic.
```

The wife doesn't hesitate. She is *hungry*. She bites in.

WIFE

```
Yes.
```

NICE NEIGHBOUR

```
It will cost you.
```

The nice old neighbour is of course a witch, didn't you know? For you can't have demonic disturbances without a little help from a witch.

27

19

The next morning, my husband has no houses to show. We sit in our pyjamas in front of the TV with the Sonos speakers and the camera ready to show us the night, but we don't have the courage to hit play yet. I feel I must warn him. Instead, we google it and it turns out worms sleep, but not necessarily how humans sleep. 'What were you really doing outside last night?' my husband asks nervously. 'Who were you talking to?' 'Here.' I hand him a copy of the screenplay I finished moments before he woke. 'Can we do a table read?' 'Now?' He is surprised. 'Now.' It must be now, for we don't have much time left.

20

We have arrived at the **SHOWDOWN**. The wife stands up from the breakfast table. Fruit rolls from her body. The suave husband rubs her shoulder consolingly. The husband of the errant blowjob is frantic.

```
        HUSBAND OF THE ERRANT BLOWJOB
        We have to run!
```

The wife crosses the kitchen serenely, as if he's telling her how good a day it would be for a picnic. Blueberries squish beneath her heels.

```
        HUSBAND OF THE ERRANT BLOWJOB
        Snap out of it, Louise! We
```

```
have to get away from that,
that, demon!
```

The wife lifts her hand. With a cupping motion — as though dipping into a bowl of chocolate pudding, as though revelling in the joy that is chocolate pudding she could not help but take a handful — she scoops out his chest. His heart. The husband of the errant blowjob is not solid, but gives in: skin and bones and blood. He stares disbelieving at the hole in his chest. With a tentative tongue, the wife tastes: his quivering flesh is sweet. She gobbles up his heart. She sucks her fingers clean.

```
HUSBAND OF THE ERRANT BLOWJOB
          (beseeching)
Louise, I believed in you.
```

She falls on him, devouring his delicious body and his scrumptious screams. The camera pans to the wife's paintings in the living room: all those dreary demons are actually sun-kissed, muscly versions of the husband. Like Roman statues, such worshiping of the male body. You see, we started the movie in the husband's perspective and now we are in the wife's. It is the **REALISATION** and the **TWIST** all in one.

21

When we finish reading my new screenplay out loud, my husband is silent. He runs his hand over and over his mouth. He keeps his eyes on the title page, as though the text might rearrange itself. 'Do you at least like the ending?' I ask. 'I think the ending is clever.' After the wife eats up the husband of the errant blowjob, the wife and the suave husband make out on the kitchen table, amidst the fruit, which flashes to wormies, which flashes to fruit, wormies, fruit, wormies, fruit. Suddenly, CUT TO BLACK. But we linger in the audio. Their heavy breathing, the wife's orgasmic moans, her shouts of exhilaration – or is that panic? Hard to tell the difference between ecstasy and terror. Then THE END. 'I think the ending is clever,' I repeat uncertainly. My husband asks, 'What did it cost?' I play dumb, 'What?' He motions in the direction of our nice neighbour's house. 'This is it, isn't it? The script that a millionaire exec will pick up? You made a deal. I know your writing. I know your stories. The first drafts are never good.' I do not argue; I rub his shoulder consolingly. 'Louise, I believed in you,' he beseeches. 'What did it cost?' He's watched enough horror movies, read enough of my horror screenplays, to already know this was coming. I pick up my husband's hand, quivering now, as insubstantial now as pudding. I do not know how to tell him I gobbled up his heart, and I am still hungry. Ravenous. So I hit play on the camera instead. The video starts with us lying down in bed, facing each other symbolically in the dark. My past self pops up and waves at the screen, at the future me, the me that is now. My husband shivers. 'You're giving me the creeps,' he says. His video past self echoes, 'You're giving me the creeps.' 'Shh,' I whisper. 'Watch.' The camera holds for so long it feels intrusive, watching ourselves as we try to sleep. Restlessly at first, shifting blankets and juggling pillows. Then my husband snores softly. I whimper. Suddenly, as if time jumped, I stand on my husband's side of the bed. I lean over him.

FRÉDÉRIC MATHIEU

E D E N
ON THE
F A R
S I D E

There is a place, high in the Andes, where men and women can go to have their futures told to them. It is a seven-day hike to the lip of the mountain and it is said that there, just below the summit, there is a man whose age no one knows who will look into your eyes and tell you what lies ahead for you. No one can say how long he has lived there, or how it is that he survives. The locals speak of him in hushed tones, bowing their heads close to your ear as they whisper to you the place — under heavy trees and by a stream running green. There is no guide. You have to take the journey alone.

At least, that was how my father always told the story. That beginning I will never forget. When he was young, very young, he was travelling through South America and he went to see the old man. He would tell me this story when we went hiking – four times a year, once per season. When we were around halfway up a hill, he would start to tell his story.

It was never the same twice. Sometimes, on sunny days, with Tollymore Forest Park stretched out below us, the mountains had been green and lush, with the sun dripping off their edges. He'd trekked through jungles and waded through rivers which flowed fast around his waist. Other times, when I had fallen and had scuffed my hands on the gravelled path we were walking, the mountains were a labyrinth of razor sharp rocks – most of his seven days were spent inching along cliff faces, watching stones skittering over the edge and dropping down onto the boulders below at every slight misstep.

When I was seven, I looked up the Andes on the computer at school and when I came home I asked him why in his stories there was never any snow at the top of the mountain and he stared at me like I had sworn at him. A few months later, when he told the story its climax was a final day of walking across a glacier, which finally gave way to the running water and vegetation that was promised – a sort of Eden on the far side of the desert.

What he found at the top varied, too. Once, as I ran my hands along a wall that had been built to pen in sheep, it was a man in an old stone hut, all the rocks piled so carefully that they needed nothing to bind them together, so skilled had been the masters who had made them. The man had dark, stick-straight hair that fell to his waist, and a hard, strong face, like a man right amidst his life. It was only the depth of his gaze that betrayed him. When we climbed Cuilcagh, the stairs at the end of the boardwalk reminded my father of the one thousand hand-carved stone steps he had been forced to climb to reach the summit of the mountain, and how he had been astounded by the almost palatial temple he found there. This time, the man had yellow teeth and appeared to be nothing more than bones, but when he took my father's hands in his there was a sinewy strength that surprised him, and his eyes had seen more than one lifetime.

But one thing all the stories had in common: my father never told me what the old man said to him, although I asked him every time. The story ended when he stopped talking, and he would never answer any questions about it, even when I told him that something had not made sense.

Our hikes were never as exciting as his through the Andes – most often he would take me to the Mournes or the Belfast hills. Still, as a child, I would hardly be able to sleep the night before we went. I would wake before the sun and rush into my father's room, throwing myself across him, shouting, 'It's time to get up, Dad!' He would nod his head with his eyes closed and tell me to go to the kitchen for breakfast.

As I grew older, the hikes meant less to me, and it became necessary instead for my father to wake me. I would sit in the pre-dawn grey of the kitchen shivering into my bowl of cereal, while he made us the same packed lunch that characterised my entire school life – ham and cheese sandwiches on wholegrain bread. My father was not a man of great culinary achievement. Birthday cakes were bought, not made. Most nights, our dinner table was set with pesto pasta, the pasta invariably overcooked. An oven pizza was my father's idea of a special meal.

The only exceptions to my father's inaptitude were on the evenings after our hikes. The night before, he would begin preparing his speciality – empanadas – so that they would be ready when we arrived back on the following day. I would watch from the doorway of the kitchen in fascination at the intense care with which he would prepare them – the almost tender way his hands would mould the dough, his knuckles flexing back and forth in a smooth rhythm, the delicacy with which the knife slipped through the onion, and his light touch when he scraped it into the pan. Those empanadas were the best thing I have ever tasted, and on those evenings we two would sit in the silence of our hunger, the only sounds the sounds of chewing, of cutlery and baked dough coming apart in our hands, our mouths. It helped that we were starving. Those evenings were really the only time I ever saw my father smile openly. I asked him once if he had learned to make the empanadas when he had been in South America. His smile faded and he nodded slowly and would answer no more questions about it.

The last time my father ever told me his story, we were walking up Slieve Donard from Newcastle and he was dying. He was dying too young – I was only twenty two then – but that was it, he was dying. I had moved out by this time but had been staying with him a lot, and on that morning I let him sleep a little longer while I made our lunches, layering sliced ham and cheddar and cutting diagonally across, drawing the knife in a smooth movement. When my father came into the kitchen, I saw his hands were shaking. I told him we didn't have to go that day but he just looked at me and so I nodded and put the backpacks in the car.

We walked up from Donard car park towards the quarry, stepping over the twisted roots of trees grown deep into the hillside, our feet cushioned by the bed of pine needles that lay there year-round. We took the straight path up the hill in silence, eschewing the winding gravel road that led up to the quarry in slow, gentle loops for the rocks and stones and a stream feeding the Shimna river, which in turn tore its way down the mountain. This was all so familiar to me I barely heard the water falling, falling in its own desperate leaps, running from the tip of the mountain as though afraid of it. The water pounded on the rocks, running brown over the coarse stones beneath it, but I did not look at it. My eyes stayed firmly fixed on my father's back, leading me up this mountain, as he must have a dozen times before. The river roared alongside us but we did not hear it, taking slow, deep-breathed steps up the slope in silence. I was listening carefully to his breathing, alert to the fact that it seemed to be getting deeper.

We worked our way up and towards the edge of the treeline, the first and easiest part of the journey done, and turned our feet sharply onto the crisp, white-dusted path that leads up to the Saddle – the ridge that connects Slieve Donard and Slieve Commedagh. This great bow rose in the air above us and behind it the blue sky silhouetted the shape of the hills. The sun engulfed the land in its brightness and the slopes shone green. This was the kind of day on which my father's hills would have been swathed in jungle, and the trees would have hung heavy with fruit so ripe their sweet juices would have run down him as he walked below them. In the last few years, he had been telling more and more elaborate versions of the tale, as though more desperate with each telling.

I worried now about the sun on my father's exposed scalp. His hair had been fair, and his pale skin burnt easily, and I had not seen him put on sunscreen that day. My own dark hair and features were so different from his that we were rarely taken to be father and son. I watched the sun strike him, so bright against his thinning frame and the skin pulled tightly over his skull. He looked almost translucent, as though it had already happened.

The hike to the summit of Slieve Donard is an easy one for any experienced hiker. If you take it slowly, it takes less than three hours up and two down. As we began to make the climb up to the Saddle, I heard his breathing begin to deepen, and as we reached the real foot of the Saddle and the steps became shorter and steeper, a ragged edge crept into his breaths. I asked him if he wanted to stop but he said nothing, stepping ahead of me.

I took a deep, impatient breath and looked away from him and back over the way we had come, the stream cutting down the hillside and the white stones that lined the path back to the trees. It looked small from here, such a little distance to have caused such pain. I followed my father. The climb began to pull at my calves, a gentle ache spreading its way up my Achilles and through my leg. I could see my father beginning to shake, and each step was exerted with a heavy breath, stamped into the ground. My throat began to burn and he seemed to move faster, breaths coming quickly and beginning to have a wet, rough sound to them. My father had just turned forty one. The climb should have been easy for him.

Up in the Saddle, he broke down. He collapsed to the ground, and I rushed forward to catch him. He sat on the grass, his breath rushing in and out of him in great heaves while I stood and stared at him. My father worked in insurance. He was a safe, stable man. When he smiled, it was a brief, small movement and he showed no teeth. I sat down beside him and saw only now the cold sweat on his brow. He would not stop shaking.

From where we sat, the mountains formed a kind of V-shape, pointing our eyes down at the treeline, and down beyond that, Newcastle sat darkly against its own white beach and the sea.

'It isn't true,' he said, and he grimaced.

'What isn't?' I said. We rarely looked each other in the eye and now his gaze would not leave mine.

'It isn't true,' he said again. 'I didn't go and see him.'

'Dad, it's okay.' I put my hand on his shoulder.

'No, listen to me. It isn't true.'

'Dad, I know—'

'Listen to me.' He looked at me until I backed off, holding my hands in the air. He kept his eyes on me as he struggled to his feet, and the expression on his face told me not to help him. I looked away from him and took a deep breath in and out. He nodded over my shoulder and I turned to look up at the summit of Slieve Donard, reaching above us. He began to cough and would not stop, retching up something on the grass. He wiped his mouth with the back of his hand and then he began, almost stumbling, to walk the final, hardest stretch of the mountain, up to the peak. And then he told me the story again.

I remember he began it the way he always began, with the myth: *There is a place, high in the Andes...* and then he told me a version I had never heard before.

'After three days I was lost. I was stupid, so young and so stupid, to wander off into the mountains without a guide. Without a guide, without a map, without anything but a legend to follow – a fairy tale I had been excited about for half a day.' A rare laugh escaped him. 'Don't look at me like that. I know you don't believe the story of me being told my future by some holy man at the top of the world, so let's see if you believe this: I gave up. I was exhausted. I had run out of water and had wasted half a day chasing what I thought was the sound of a river running down the mountain and found nothing. I swear I heard it though, as clearly as you hear water rushing down that hill.' He closed his eyes and shrugged. 'It doesn't matter anymore.'

He stopped for a moment, resting his hands heavily on the stone wall that runs the length of the mountain, from the Saddle to its peak. His breathing was harsh and he looked very pale.

'I gave up. There wasn't a moment where it happened – I just stopped, somewhere in the forest, and then I turned around and began to walk back down.'

We began walking again and he was silent for a while but I did not say anything. For the first time in years, I wanted to listen to him. What else did he say? He told me of how he walked and walked – it didn't matter much the way he walked because all that he wanted was to go down, to get out of those mountains, to feel the ground flat under his feet again. He was so desperate that he walked into the night and when it came, cool and blue, he kept walking, barely awake, barely sane. He could not feel his feet anymore. It had been a long time since I had been able to see what my father saw and a long time since I had been able to feel what he felt.

We stopped again, my father stumbling, and me reaching out to hold him up. We were close to the top, but my father could not see it – he was looking out towards the sea. From this side of the mountain we were on the wrong side of it – from there you could see Newcastle, and the sea at its side stretching up to the north, but you couldn't see the whole thing. He kept talking.

There was a moment where he was not sure it would ever end, this walk down, always down. Through a gap in the trees he saw the ocean – the Pacific – stretching off under the moon-light. He could see a bay that he was in, with the water running itself right up against the mountains on its far side, and the blue stars glancing off the ocean on their way past the horizon. The sea was rising to meet him, transforming into mist before his eyes and rolling up into the mountains. It looked so cool, so clear. He walked to meet it and it was all lost again in the trees.

My father's gaze seemed to sweep around and catch itself on the mountain in its way, and he began to walk again. This time, he let me help him. We walked slowly together. We have so few words for pain.

When we crested the hill, he let me go again, and I was afraid that he would fall, but he stood there, shaking on his own legs, like a child learning to walk. He staggered to the far side of the summit and I watched him go, as he had let me make my own way once too. Finally, I went to stand at his shoulder and we both looked out. Now you could see the sea truly, one clear breath wrapping itself around the coast, and to the south you could see it driving in towards Carlingford Bay, glittering under the sun.

He reached the bottom at dawn, and he came out of the trees in the early morning mist, out from under the heavy branches and into a clearing in a valley – and there she was.

'There was who?'

'A woman,' he said, 'a woman washing clothes in a green stream.' I had never seen this expression on his face before.

It's hard to remember now, how much of this he told me, and how much of it I just saw through him. I could have asked him then, I'm sure I could have, what happened next:

She had seen him and her eyes had widened and she had come towards him, almost afraid – he must have looked half dead. She was the most beautiful creature he had ever seen. She had brown eyes that took away everything else. She had taken his hands and hers had been so dark against his. He had seen his future in front of him; he had known it then – as clearly as though she was telling him.

And if he told me this, I'm sure I asked him the question that I always asked him every time—

'What did she tell you?'

And if I asked him, he would have told me. There is so much I don't remember now. So much of him I have forgotten. I was so young then and so afraid.

The sun was endless at the top of Slieve Donard. Below us the land stretched away forever in one direction, full of everything, and the empty sea stretched away forever in the other. My father would not take his eyes off it.

ANNA NÍ DHÚILL

I GET ALONG WITHOUT YOU VERY WELL

I wonder if she knows I'm watching her listen. My phone screen lights up, notifying me of rain sounds playing on a speaker halfway across the world. It is my mid-morning, her midnight. I look down at the phone as God might His universe, a big-faced child staring down at its freshly dead fish's bowl. Watching my phone play thunder I picture her so perfectly; perfect in her smugness and snugness and inability to sleep.

Maybe this is just what a modern break-up looks like. Digital stalking, unfolding in real-time, the stalker unwilling but made to become this doomed stereotype. She has made me a perpetrator, despite the fact that she is half-asleep and I am in another country. I hide my phone quickly, so the girls working won't see, hoping that my reactivity will be pocketed along with it. They would say I'm overreacting: you knew already she'd be asleep, she's in California, why be struck down now, it's been months, don't spiral, you owe it to yourself to be over it by now. All of a sudden, I get a hot flash and quickly rise from my desk to bolt to the bathroom. I lock myself in a cubicle and make no sound, just sit on the folded-down lid and stare at the phone. All of my attention directed at this screen and yet I vividly imagine us, me and her, at either end of an impossibly long table. Is this rain sound our peace treaty? Where do I sign?

After surviving particularly well the past five months of zero-contact, I'm beginning to feel the corporeal heat of her emotional growth. She is forgetting me. She does not know that my hair is in a mullet, or that I'm on a salary now, or that I still want to be remembered. Has it only taken that long for her to have boxed up all of my belongings and unboxed them all again, to have suppressed, even, that they belong to me? And then to begin getting *use* out of them? That's *my* Alexa that's providing you with a tranquil night's sleep. It is *me* curating your dreams, you know.

That last bit sounds good to me. It is only now that I realise I am in control; I have playlist power. I am MC Bygone, DJ Left Behind. My stage name is The Sleep Disruptor. Taking a deep breath I decide there are two ways this could go: I put my cards on the table and choose a song from our shared past, or I go full heavy-metal and draw a line in the sand. The former takes from me the last five months of healing, the latter is an opportunity to limit any reconciliation of friendship in the future. I choose "Hello", by Adele. No meaning behind it, just politely flagging my presence and maybe giving her a chuckle out of it. Leaving the bathroom cubicle with unjustifiable adrenaline, I tell my reflection telepathically that she'll probably sleep through it. Adele's voice is nothing if not soothing.

My co-workers take no aim at my extended bathroom visit, so I sit quietly back in front of my computer and mindlessly begin replying to an email with lalalalalalalala. This not only is an unhelpful distraction for me, but provides no information for Kevin on what time would be best for him to call in and collect his keys from the lost and found. Curbing my guilt about being a terrible employee, I Ctrl+Z and let him know someone will be in the office until seven this evening, all the best. Upon completion, I whip out my phone over-conspicuously to check for an anthemic response. Adele has finished, and it seems she has sung us both out. There is no soundtrack to our reunion, only ringing phones and the sound of staplers on my end, and an apparently successful night's sleep on hers.

I have my answer; she does not know I'm here, watching the soundtrack to her sleep, waiting for her to play this game with me. This is a sign that is was *not* a sign, nor an instigation, but an act of forgetting what was once the most important love on the planet. If I don't laugh I'll cry, so I put on "you up?" by Yaya Bey (one of her favourites), and I play it on her speaker, and smile at the memory of her putting on this album for me for the first time. And I have done this way too often: recalling our time together perhaps as a form of self-harm, to remind myself that I had the most magical, unattainable love, and now all I have is my annual salary. I do this, go through our timeline, comb through each conversation. I accept that I have pain to face without fully accepting the pain itself; I am constantly aware that I am being forgotten and less aware that I, myself, am forgetting. Because, if I'm forgetting, then surely it wasn't as all-consuming as I believe? Here it comes again, that heatwave, until–

I look down at my screen

and I haven't even noticed that

my phone, on her speaker, is playing "What's Up?" by the 4 Non Blondes.

Relief is a flood washing through my body and my temperature returns to normal.

The phone rings and offers me a moment of emotional regulation, safe from the oscillating highs and lows. It's Kevin, god bless him, ringing to say he'll be here to collect his keys at five, he wonders if this is too late and if it definitely suits us all in the office, because if it doesn't just let him know, because the last thing he wants to be is a pest when he knows we're all very busy here. Don't be worrying Kevin, I say, myself and Kirsty are rostered on till 7 this evening because there's this big project we're working on. He asks me about the project and I oblige, but more than that, I am *thriving* at small talk. We're in the middle of discussing our morning routines when I remember the reason for my manic happiness, glance at my phone which is now playing Phoebe Bridgers' "I See You". I wait for Kevin to finish up and let him know I'll see him later, hang up the phone, and make a mental list of all appropriate and humorous song titles I could respond with.

I choose "How are Things in Glocca Morra?" by Petula Clark and Fred Astaire.

My imagination has me wreathed in smiles thinking about her searching for context. Laughing at her laughing at the terrible accent, thinking about her thinking about the many times we sang along to her warped record of *Downtown,* her only frame of reference for this song.

She throws back an easy "California Dreamin'" .

Offended, almost, at the lack of thought on her part, I put on "The Less I Know the Better". I panic she won't understand that I'm being facetious through all these devices when she returns with "Alone Again (Naturally)". I realise I'm missing out on the full experience, so I stick my headphones in the computer in front of me and click Gilbert O'Sullivan's YouTube channel. It's the first time I really listen to the lyrics, and I realise that it's not the melodramatic song I always pegged it as, but rather about how he mourned his parents' death.

O'Sullivan has changed the game for me. He takes me out of my online streaming romance predicament and places me back in my reality: I'm in my workplace, I'm supposed to be focusing on a very important project, and I'm clearly still in love with my ex-girlfriend.

"All Good?" De La Soul and Chaka Khan slice through my silence. She doesn't like being left on read, or whatever the equivalent is in this damned mousetrap game we had silently entered into. Invoking the spirit of Gilbert, I muster all my courage in one big spiritual embrace and play "I Think It's Going to Rain Today".

Not the Judy Collins cover, or the Nina Simone version, or even the original, which was written by Randy Newman in 1966, she told me once. None of those – I play the Dave Van

Ronk version. Our favourite. The one we were going to play at our wedding. For a fictitious event, we had it immaculately planned, and discussed in detail. Perhaps choosing such a bleak song for our imaginary first dance was a bad omen. But that just added to the nicheness, the intimacy of our familiarity with each other. We were bonded so elementally that when we found this song one morning the world stopped and enveloped us and spat out all the fatty bits, the bits unnecessary to me and you.

The song plays out. A few seconds go by and

"Can I Call You Tonight?"

before waiting for an answer, she changes to

"Gay Thoughts", and I laugh.

There is a twisted part of me that is glowing in the knowledge that she still thinks of me. The hollowness I feel in not being around her doesn't feel tragic or painful, but like an honour. She made me giddy, she made me so strong. There was nothing negative in our relationship except the feeling of wanting to give more. To shower her in haikus, to buy her lunch at Blue Danube, cookies at Milk, McDonald's on whatever corner she happened to get hungry at. To make her laugh harder. To make her understand the importance of her life in the grand scheme of everything.

As much as I love this feeling of being known, of being metaphysically held steady in a universe in flux, I know that above all else there is no going backwards. And I hope that doesn't mean that we never speak again, or stop sending each other songs we think the other would like, or that one day we feel no feeling at all for one another. Because the immense swell of love I have for you is exhilarating. And I know it won't always be like that, or can't, because we can't be in love any more, because you're there and I'm here, but oh my god, you have changed me as a human and I have learned so many things from you. To have known you is a gift and to have been loved by you has been the highlight of my life. So, while we were not made to love each other forever, I do hope I know you forever.

That's what I said to her when she called me that evening. She described her new apartment in San Francisco: the multi-coloured woven rug we got at a flea market, modern greyish furnishings, the blackout blinds she got installed to help with the insomnia. There's too much space for just one person — which is very cruel, she says, given the recent separation from the woman she loves. But it's not that recent, really, anymore. I don't say that out loud, because of course it is a consolation for my benefit. But we both think it. I suggest she get a cat, and she reminds me she's allergic. I guess I forgot.

She reset the speaker that night so that she could listen to rain sounds without disturbing me again. After we cried over the phone and parted painfully once more, I sent her a playlist of some of our favourite songs from over the years. I called it "What'll I Do?", after the Sinatra song. A few days later, I texted to see if she had listened to it yet, and if she had enjoyed it. She sent back a link to Chet Baker's song "Get Along Without You Very Well" as sole response.

BEAN SÍ

A bitter wind blew through the bare branches of the oak tree in the front field. Cáit shivered, drawing her black woollen shawl tighter around her shoulders. Her white-knuckled fingers worried at the knots along its fringe. Micheál stood before her, his cheeks ruddy against the afternoon chill. The sounds of mooing, snorting, and squelching in mud drifted up the bóithrín from the road beyond. Micheál's brother Seán stamped his feet alongside the herd to keep the blood flowing while he waited.

'Put a bit of a hurry on yourself, will you?' he called to his brother, brow furrowing in annoyance.

Micheál turned to his troubled wife.

'Micheál, please… I don't want to be here alone. Send someone else. They can surely spare you this once.'

He sighed wearily. 'It isn't this once, though, is it? It's all the times I haven't left since… well. And it's all the trips to come. It's time, Cáit. And look, it's only for the night. I'll be back before lunch tomorrow. You'll hardly even know I'm gone.'

He gently took his wife's chin and tilted her head to look up at him. Cáit jerked it away without meeting his eyes. She folded her arms, wrapping her shawl even tighter.

In truth, Micheál was looking forward to getting away from her, to losing himself in the bottom of a pint and laying aside his worries for a few precious hours. His wife was so deep in her grief that there was no space left for his. There hadn't been in some time. Still, seeing her so fearful, even knowing, as he did, that the fear was of her own making, made his chest tighten. But the cattle had to be brought to the mart, and his brother refused to do the two-man job alone.

'It'll all be fine, a chroí,' he murmured, wrapping his arms around Cáit's hunched shoulders. 'You'll see.'

She drew back into herself and away from him, and he felt the distance keenly. So much distance, of late. His arms fell to his sides as his wife's chill cooled his own heart.

'You've enough to be doing to keep yourself busy, anyway, haven't you? The water needs to be drawn, and you'll soon be having to fix yourself some dinner. And, sure, there's plenty of cleaning to be done if you find yourself idle.'

Cáit's eyes narrowed, and her chin puckered. 'Well, if you're going, then off with you. I've enough to be at, as you said. Go on away with you, now!'

Micheál shook his head and made his way down the bóithrín to the road. Himself, his brother, and their small herd departed amidst "gits" and "hyups" and bass lowing. Cáit watched them go until the whistling wind swallowed their noise, and she was all that was left.

She turned to the empty farmhouse, its windows shining in the flat winter sun. Behind it was the familiar dense thicket of trees disappearing into the distance. It looked dark today. Foreboding, somehow. Cáit wondered what was out there, lurking in the shadows between the trees. Her fingers sought out the fringe of her shawl once more.

I have enough to be doing to keep me busy.

The front door caught on the rough flagstone floor, grinding in its usual way. The resulting screech set Cáit's nerves on end. A curved scuff had formed there over time. Cáit could sometimes make out shapes in the little bumps and sweeping grooves; things stuck in the tiles which came alive by her noticing.

She averted her eyes now. The house was dark today. It felt heavy.

That scuff, though. How long had it been since she had cleaned the floor, anyway?

Too long. Perhaps a lick of polish will keep the door from catching.

Soon, she was on all fours, a bucket of soapy water beside her, a wooden scrubber clasped in both hands. She went at the scuff with the ire of a personal vendetta, and she didn't stop there. By the time she was done, the hall, sitting room, and kitchen floors had all been scoured with an attention to detail that bordered on the obsessive. Every scrub of the rough brush seemed to push the things that lived in the flagstone further from her view.

Then came the polish. Cáit used an old mop to spread the dark and viscous liquid over the scuffed floor. The flagstone drank up the much-needed tonic, and the scuff began to fade, though it did not disappear entirely. Cáit grumbled under her breath. It would need a second coat. The rest of the hall got the same treatment. The acrid polish tickled the back of Cáit's throat as she worked, and by the time she had finished with the sitting room, her head was swimming from the fumes.

She left the polish and the mop out – she'd get back to that later – and made her way to the kitchen. She slumped into one of the kitchen chairs and leaned against the table, resting her head in the crook of her arm for just a few moments.

Cáit decided she would take the evening off from cooking; sure, why go to the bother of making a whole meal for just herself? A bit of fresh bread would do, warm from the oven with the neighbour's butter and the blackcurrant jam she'd made last September. There was still some left. It was lasting longer than she had expected. But then, of course it would. There was one less mouth to draw from it.

She gathered the ingredients – the flour, the buttermilk, the baking soda. She took out the cast iron pot that had been a gift from her aunt when she had married Micheál. It was well-seasoned now, and the bread that came out of it was second to none.

Cáit soon began to lose herself in the making of the bread, in the sensory feast of measuring, mixing, and kneading. She had always loved baking. As a child, she would watch her grand-mother's practiced hands and help where she could. There was a little magic, she thought, in creating something new and deli-cious from a set of inert elements.

She slid the pot full of pale dough into the waiting aga stove and stood in front of it for a moment as though on standby. She was unsure what she should do next. Her hands were quiet, and her mind was suddenly loud in the stillness of the empty farmhouse.

She could go to the well. She *should* go to the well. But she didn't want to. She didn't like going through the thicket of trees. There were things out there, she was sure of it. She could feel their eyes on her as they watched her. They were waiting for something.

Waiting for me to join them in the darkness. Waiting for me to let them in.

Cáit shook herself and chuckled nervously at her own morbidity. Micheál would say it was just a feeling, and that feeling something didn't make it real. Anyway, she'd used the last of the water cleaning the floors. She'd want some for tea later, and Micheál would be angry at her if the first thing he had to do upon his return was to make the trip himself. So, she set aside her misgivings, grabbed the two large pails sitting by the back door, and wrapped her shawl around her shoulders once more.

Cáit sang to herself as she trudged down the muddy track between trees, branches trembling above her in the breeze. It was a melancholy melody – one her mother used to sing to her when she was small. Her mother had loved sad songs. She'd died when Cáit was a wean. An accident on the farm, her father would say, and little else on the subject.

It was all shadows in the wood, the trees were growing so dense. Cáit thought for a moment that she saw something move. It lurked at the edges of her peripheral vision, just out of sight. When she tried to look at it head-on, there was nothing but moss-covered tree trunks and thorny shrubbery glistening from the earlier rain. The air was alive with the smell of wet greenery and damp earth.

Cáit quickened her pace. She didn't want to linger.

Soon, she came upon the well in its little clearing. It was a beautiful place, this. Haunting, but beautiful. A sense of quiet and mystery rose up within her when her gaze fell upon the old stone ruin, all but swallowed up now by the wood around it, and the small mound that curved behind the well, with the little bushes dotted uniformly around it.

Cáit shuddered.

She approached the low stone wall marking the edge of the well and set down one of the pails. She swung a leg over the wall and steadied her foothold before reaching to dip the other pail into the dark mirror.

As the bucket breached the surface and water began to gush in, Cáit felt a hot breath against the back of her neck. The hair there stood on end and shivers ran the length of her body. The sound of lips pulling back and stretching over teeth whispered wetly in her right ear. She gasped and instinctively hunched her shoulder against the sound, twisting around to see its maker.

There was no one there.

The momentum of Cáit's rapid turn made her lose her foothold and stumble forward into the well. There was a great splash as her body hit the dark reservoir of water — water that was cold enough to steal the air from her lungs and the blood from her extremities.

Her dress quickly became sodden. She had to get out before it became so waterlogged that it pulled her into the depths of the well. She kicked hard against the water, trying to keep her head above it. Her breath came in short, panicked bursts as she grasped for the edge of the well. Once she found it, she heaved with all her strength and managed to pull herself out of the water.

She lay beside the well for a moment, trying to steady her breath and slow her pounding heart, but her body was still abuzz with adrenaline. She struggled to her feet under the weight of the wet dress and looked around once more. There was no one in the clearing but her. And yet, she couldn't shake the feeling that someone – some*thing* – was watching her. She shivered, more from fear than from the unrelenting chill.

The fear soon turned to shame.

Cop on – you're the only one here! You're lucky no one else was here to see this… These nerves will be the death of you.

Cáit couldn't help but wonder, in her morbid way, what it would have felt like to die in that well, falling through the darkness as her body screamed from the cold and the lack of air until it finally went numb. How long would it have taken Micheál to find her? The first pail had fallen into the well alongside her. The only clue that she had been there was the second pail still sitting beside the wall, waiting to be filled.

She sighed. Might as well get what she came for. She took more care this time, kneeling beside the well, planting herself firmly before she dipped the pail in. The clearing was still. *Too still*, she might have thought, were she not relieved at the very lack of sound. The denizens of the wood had fallen silent. Even the wind had died down.

Cáit rose and trudged through the clearing, lopsided with the weight of the pail, and started down the muddy path to the farmhouse. Her dress stuck to her skin and bunched uncomfortably between her legs.

The back of her neck began to prickle once more.

Goose pimples sprang up over her body.

An ear-splitting shriek tore through the wood.

Cáit froze, her heartbeat a drum against the roof of her mouth, and slowly turned around. Something was standing in the heart of the clearing. It was grotesquely tall and thin, with skeletal arms that reached down past its knees. Sagging breasts drooped from a sunken chest. A grimy silken shift hung from its withered body, and a moth-bitten veil covered long, grey hair that undulated gently. The creature's jaw was unhinged, the ashen skin of its face stretched taut over the bones beneath. Its piercing scream reverberated through dead air.

Cáit was gripped with a frenzy she had never felt before, and a scream tore through her throat unbeknownst to her. It harmonized absurdly with the last echoes of the creature's own. The metal pail hit the ground with a clang, and the water inside sloshed out, puddling on the muddy path. Cáit ran, and kept on running, and did not look back. She fancied she saw the tree roots snaking their way out of the underbrush, trying to trip her and drag her into the depths of the forest. Trying to trap her there.

She reached the edge of the wood, and the farmhouse came into sight. Dusk was near, falling quicker than she had expected. The forest behind her was growing foggy and inscrutable in the waning light. The creature was nowhere to be seen.

It's still there. Hiding. Just out of sight.

She hurried back to the house in case it decided to show itself once more. She locked the doors and drew all the curtains, almost tripping over the forgotten mop and bucket as she entered the living room.

The house felt cold and eerie. Cáit busied herself with laying a fire. Her hands were shaking still, and the match kept slipping. She cursed under her breath, dropped the matches entirely, choked back tears, then – finally – a *hiss* and a *snap* and the match was lit. She held it to the tinder, and tiny flames began to flicker underneath the turf.

Cáit sat back on her haunches and watched the embryonic fire grow. It occurred to her that she hadn't gotten the very thing she had gone into the woods for – the water. She cursed again. She'd do without. Micheál would have to fetch some when he returned. Let him deal with whatever horror lived in the clearing. Cáit swore she would never set foot near that well again.

She imagined what her husband would think when she told him. He would say she was imagining things again. Even now, in the warm glow of the fire and safe in her home, Cáit wondered if any of it had happened at all; but her doubt soon waned under the weight of memory, under the visceral fear that brought ice to her veins even now. She thought of the fairy fort behind the well and of the *Aos Sí* that were rumoured to live beneath such places.

A Bean Sí. What else could that thing be?

Some said that the wail of the *Bean Sí* warned of an impending death in the family. Well, if that were the case, then it – *she* – was about five months too late.

Cáit suddenly became acutely aware of the cold, wet dress that still clung to her trembling body. She hurried to the bedroom she shared with Micheál and peeled it off, catching a glimpse of herself in the large oval mirror that stood in the corner of the room as she did. Waxy skin with a winter pallor, sunken eyes underlined by dark crescent moons, a downturned mouth, and dry, cracked lips. She threw the wet dress over the mirror to hide the reflection and wrapped herself in a nightgown. As she softened into its fluffy embrace, she became aware of an acrid burning smell, one she hadn't noticed upon entering, so preoccupied was she with what had happened at the well.

The soda bread!

Cáit ran to the kitchen, the freshly polished hall floor sticking a little on the soles of her bare feet. The aga stove was spewing dark grey smoke, rendering the kitchen as opaque as the forest outside. Cáit coughed and sputtered as she opened the stove and, hands covered in thick oven mitts, withdrew the smouldering loaf.

She opened the back door and flung the charred mess into the backyard as she howled in frustration. Nerves and smoke had her eyes welling up with tears. She left the back door open for a time and sat at the kitchen table, resting her head in the crook of her arms once more. The smoke swirled around her and she felt its weight fill her lungs. She wanted to hide within it. But it soon cleared, and Cáit closed the door behind it.

She returned to the sitting room and curled up in Micheál's favourite armchair, hugging her knees close to her chest. The fire was blazing now, and she gazed unblinkingly into it. She felt numb. The adrenaline that had spurred her on thus far had run out, and she felt like there was no more fuel for feeling. She was an empty vessel. Her weary mind happily lost itself in its dancing flames.

Knock, knock, knock...

Cáit woke with a start. Had she been dreaming? She was sure she had heard something. She was still in the armchair. The fire had burned through much of the turf, and the flames had given way to glowing embers. Cáit waited and listened. Her breath was loud in the silence.

Knock, knock, knock!

The soft little raps grew louder and more insistent. Someone was at the front door. Cáit was overcome with a foreboding feeling; still, she rose from the armchair and slowly made her way towards the front door. The closer she grew to it, the louder the knocks became, until she was right in front of it, and the door was almost dancing in its jamb, shaking with the force of whatever was on the other side.

'Who's there?' Cáit had to shout to be heard above the din.

The knocking ceased, and everything grew calm, still, and quiet. Too quiet. Cáit's heart was in her mouth, a heavy unease having taken its place in her chest. She let out an uneven breath.

'Who's there?!'

The reply was instant this time, and Cáit heard it as clearly as if the speaker were right beside her, whispering into her ear.

'Let me in, mam. Please. I'm so cold...' The little voice was whining, pitiful, pleading, and it wrapped around Cáit like a vice.

'Cian? Cian, love, is that you?'

'It's so cold here. I want to come in. Let me *in*!' The small voice grew until it became a scream. The wind outside followed suit, whistling through hidden gaps in the roof and whooshing through the rafters. There was silence from beyond the door.

'…Cian? Are you still there?'

No answer.

Cáit reached out a shaky hand to open the door. She had barely touched the knob when the door burst inwards, knocking her off her feet. She hit the ground hard as the door slammed against the wall. It shuddered in place, the hinges squeaking under the strain. Winded, Cáit stumbled to her feet and looked for her son.

There was nothing out there. No sign of Cian. No sign of anything or anyone, only the rural void spreading out before her. She slowly closed the door and retreated into the sitting room. The wind eventually died down, and the house fell silent. Only the rasping of Cáit's rapid breaths filled the stagnant air of the farmhouse.

She began to rummage through the drawers of the sitting room dresser, looking for a set of rosary beads she knew was around somewhere. She found them beneath some old farm ledgers and began counting the beads. Her hands steadied as they caressed the cool glass.

'*Ár nAthair, atá ar neamh…*'

The ritual words felt strange and uncomfortable in her mouth, unpractised as she was, but she said them anyway. She was halfway through a decade of the rosary when another sound joined her murmurings: a gentle creaking drifting in from the hall. Cáit fell silent and turned slowly, dread closing its iron fist around her throat. She crept to the doorway of the sitting room and peeked around the corner to see the cellar door swinging slowly open.

She knew she shouldn't go into the cellar. She didn't want to. She was afraid of what she would find. But she had to; Cian was down there.

She was beginning to think he had never left.

Cian's laughter bubbled in that youthful, infectious way as he pulled at Cáit's apron strings. She laughed alongside him. Sunlight spilled into the kitchen, refracting through rain droplets that still clung to the glass. Cáit wiped her floured hands against her apron and whipped around, arms outstretched in the promise of a tickle. Cian's curls bounced as he escaped her grasp. His laugh erupted once more as he ran giddily out of the kitchen and around the corner. Then a thump, a dull crack, and a soft little gasp. The laughter cut off abruptly.

'Cian?' Cáit called from the kitchen. No answer.

'Cian, love, are you alright?' Still nothing. Cáit's blood began to run cold, and she dashed out into the hall. The cellar door was open, and Cáit approached it on legs that had turned liquid, knowing without seeing what awaited her there.

But Cian wasn't crumpled awkwardly at the foot of the stairs now. He was standing in the far corner, his neck crooked, his head askew. He watched her unblinkingly. Tears filled Cáit's eyes as she looked upon this dark facsimile of her son, and she began to walk towards him. She bent to take him into her arms and was rewarded with a short, cool embrace. Cian pushed her away and pointed behind her.

Cáit turned to see an old, mildewed mirror reflecting a different reality. Cian was there, but Cáit wasn't. Instead, standing in her place, arm draped possessively around her son, Cáit saw the Bean Sí. The creature's mouth opened wider and wider until it was horrendously agape. A great keening filled Cáit's ears. She crumpled under its weight.

Micheál pushed open the wrought iron gate at the mouth of the bóithrín that led up to his home. He had left town at dawn, eager to return to his wife. He knew she must have suffered while he was away. The air was cold, but the day was bright, the winter sun painting everything within sight stark and silver.

The door was ajar. Micheál frowned. Cáit should know better than to leave it open like that. Who knows what critters might come in from the winter chill to take up residence in their abode? He stepped inside and closed the door behind him. He was disappointed to smell only the stale ashes from an old fire. Cáit hadn't baked him any fresh bread or gotten any breakfast ready for his return. And where was she, anyway?

'Cáit, are you up?' he called. His wife did not answer. He checked the bedroom and was surprised to see that the bed hadn't been slept in. A damp dress was hanging over the mirror in the corner.

He returned to the hall. 'Where are you, a stóirín? Don't be hiding, now. It's not funny.' He cocked his head for the slightest hint of an answer.

A low chuckle drifted towards him. He followed it to the cellar door, by which time it had dissipated once more into silence. He heaved a sigh. He hadn't liked going down there since Cian's accident – neither of them had – but, apparently, his wife was trying his patience. He knew she didn't want him to go to the mart, but he hadn't expected her to be so vindictive about it.

He descended into the cellar, his still muddy boots landing on the stairs with heavy thumps. The chuckling started up again.

'Cáit?' Micheál was growing more uneasy by the moment. A sliver of daylight shone into the cellar through the narrow little window below the ceiling. It was barely enough to see by, but it did allow Micheál to discern his wife's hunched form in front of the old mirror propped against the far wall. Its surface had been shattered, and a spiderweb pattern had spread over the glass. Large chunks had fallen from it and lay on the ground, sparkling dully in the paltry light.

'Cáit? Are you alright?' Micheál asked softly. Cáit seemed only then to become aware of his presence, and she turned to him, eyes wide and manic, face drawn. He knew this look.

Micheál opened his arms and beckoned for Cáit to come to him. She rose on shaky legs, a large shard of glass clutched in her right hand, blood running down her fingers in bright red rivulets that dripped onto the earthen floor below. Her husband did not see the glass nor the blood, so focused was he on his wife's face and so troubled was he by what he saw there.

She stepped into his embrace. Micheál took in his wife's smell as he drew her close to him. She smelled like earth and rain and green things. She was limp in his arms at first, but then one of hers snaked around his back while the other reached upwards, to caress his cheek. He liked when she did that.

Cáit slipped the shard of glass into the side of her husband's neck like a knife through butter. It slid through sinew and muscle as though it were nothing at all. Blood began to seep around the edges, and the soft flow turned to spurting little jets as Cáit removed the shard. She chuckled softly as the man she loved gurgled wordlessly.

Micheál fell to his knees as a terrible keening sound filled his ears. His eyes rolled in his head, and the last thing he saw was his wife's contorted face.

Cáit was sitting on a bench outside the facility. One of the nurses lingered nearby, ready to bring her back inside when she'd had her fill of fresh air.

She was chemically numb. For her own good, they said, and – unspoken – for everyone else's. She had been in this place with the soft rooms and steel-nerved nurses for... Well, who knew? She had lost track of time.

They told her she killed Micheál. She didn't recall. She tried to tell them about the creature – the Bean Sí. They didn't listen, just looked at her with an awful mix of pity and horror. She didn't belong here, alongside the criminals and the insane; and yet, with the cocktail of pills they were having her take, she could hardly even drum up any resentment.

Evening was approaching, and Cáit showed no sign of wanting to return indoors. The facility was near the shore, and though she could not see the ocean, she could smell its salty brine, and she savoured the scent.

Miss Dorothy eventually got sick of waiting and ushered her inside. Cáit allowed herself to be cajoled and directed. It made no difference, really, if she was inside or out. Cian was gone, and Micheál now, too. Nothing mattered anymore.

The nurse settled her into a worn armchair in the common room. Another patient walked in circles, bouncing enthusiastically on the balls of their feet and repeating words and sounds over and over as though they enjoyed the taste of them. Someone else, fancying themselves a musician, sat at the out-of-tune piano in the corner and smashed out discordant clusters of notes until one of the attendants told them off and convinced them to pursue a quieter activity for the evening.

Cáit's armchair was near a window, which began to reflect the scenes inside as the evening grew darker. She tried not to look too deeply into that other world within the window, but she couldn't help glimpsing from the corner of her eye her own reflection in the darkened glass. She couldn't help seeing the mouth stretched wide in an endless, voiceless scream.

DANIELLE MULLEN

PROSPERITY

Two weeks after Wanetta hires the new farmhand, she announces she has a horrible headache.

'I'm going to bed early,' she tells her daughter Effie. 'Be nice to Charlie at dinner.'

Charlie is the latest in the long line of strangers hired to work on Bright Farm. Once Effie turned sixteen Wanetta put up the WORKERS WANTED sign next to their mailbox. Before then, the men from town were all the help they needed.

'You know what you need to do — just get it over with,' Wanetta adds before heading upstairs.

Effie doesn't want to just "get it over with." The past few strangers were leering creeps she did her best to avoid. Charlie is kind and friendly to her. There's something sweet about him and that makes it even worse.

Dinner is a silent affair once she informs Charlie her mother is ill, and he tells her to pass on his well wishes. Effie concentrates on cutting her food, spearing bites with her fork, chewing, swallowing, and avoiding Charlie's eyes.

'Dinner is really good tonight,' he says when both their plates are nearly empty.

Effie shrugs. Her mother never compliments her cooking, but the men always do. Wanetta tells her not to believe their words and that men lie to get what they want. She knows better than to say her mother is no stranger to that kind of lying.

'You're a really good cook.'

'Mmm…' She cuts her chicken into smaller pieces.

Charlie offers to help with the dishes. She tells him she doesn't need any help, but he insists. He stacks and carries plates to the sink while she fills the washbasin with soap and water. He washes while she dries and puts away.

'What do you do when you aren't in the kitchen?' he asks.

'I like to read.' She takes her time drying a fork before placing it in the drawer.

He asks what she's reading. When she mentions there's a big family in her novel, he asks her if she wishes she had a larger family.

'Sometimes,' she looks shyly at him, 'it would be nice to have more people to talk other than Mama.'

'Ah. I had a brother. It was nice.'

She wants to ask about his brother but something about the way he says it makes her decide not to pursue the topic. After a few minutes of clanking and sloshing, she asks him if he likes to read too. When the dishes are done, they sit at the kitchen table, chatting until Effie's voice starts to fade and her eyelids droop. She apologises for keeping Charlie up so late.

'I wouldn't be here if I didn't want to be.' He smiles and she thinks he looks like a movie star. She's never been to the pictures, but she does have a stack of Modern Screen that belonged to a previous stranger. Charlie's face is thinner than any movie star she's seen, but there's something sparkling in his dark eyes that wasn't there when he first arrived at the farm.

'What happened last night?' Wanetta asks Effie the next morning.

'We washed the dishes and talked.' She looks down at her hands working over sticky bread dough. She feels her cheeks warm, and wonders if her mother will notice.

'Talked?' she sighs. 'Remember, Effie, beggars can't be choosers.'

'We aren't beggars Mama.'

'I thought that too, once.' She clicks her tongue and leaves.

Charlie insists on helping Effie with the dishes every night. She no longer cleans pots and pans as she cooks. He notices the extra work and teases her about it. They talk and talk and just when Effie worries they've run out of things to say they find a new subject. When he learns she's never seen a movie, he's shocked.

'How about I borrow that truck behind the barn and take you on Saturday?'

'No one's touched that truck since Daddy… it's been years. I don't think it runs.'

'We could walk. It's not very far.'

She shakes her head.

'What if we go outside and look at the stars instead?' he suggests.

On clear nights they look at the stars; on cloudy ones they listen to the radio. Effie reads poetry and short stories. Charlie teaches her how to dance. She mends his socks, and he brings her bunches of wildflowers.

Wanetta performs the ceremony and a quick, dry peck seals their union. Effie wears her great grandmother's dress and Charlie is in a shirt and tie he walked into town to buy. Effie makes strawberry shortcake, but barely touches it or her dinner.

It's not yet dark when they go to bed. The summer sun lights Effie's bedroom with a soft orange glow. It's the first time Charlie has been in her room, and he examines everything and asks questions. She tells him who is in the photographs on her vanity and shows him she made room in her wardrobe for his clothes. He thumbs through several of the books on her shelf while she sits at her vanity and focuses on brushing her hair. Charlie sits on the bed and takes his shoes off. He loosens his tie and starts on his shirt but stops after one button.

'We never talked about this, and we should have, but…' Charlie trails off. 'I know you want a big family, but we don't have to rush anything.'

'I don't want children… yet.'

'There are lots of things we can do that won't lead to children.' He blushes.

'I know,' she says, and he looks relieved. She supposes he expected her to be completely naive. Her mother gave her a graphic mechanical description of what would achieve pregnancy when she was fourteen. When the sons of workers joined in for harvest, she started stealing time and kisses with boys at the age of fifteen. For two years, she and Caleb Woodlee met up outside of the harvest. They took things well beyond kissing and he asked her to marry him, but her mother forbade it. She told Effie she wasn't allowed to marry a local man because it led to too many questions. Caleb is now five years married, working in his uncle's grocery, and has a son. Every now and then, Effie thinks she could have run away. Or she could have gotten pregnant and made the marriage necessary. But those ideas were just fantasies. Only a much braver person could have done such things.

'Effie?' Charlie asks. 'Are you okay?'

'Just thinking.' She lays down the brush and joins him on the bed.

Six months pass. Wanetta comes into the kitchen and watches Effie ice an applesauce cake.

'What are you baking a cake for?'

'Charlie's birthday. I'm going to hide it and then bring it out after dinner.' She smiles at her mother and Wanetta frowns.

'We shouldn't be celebrating that man. There's clearly something wrong with him. How is it that you're not pregnant?'

'These things just take time.' Effie keeps her eyes on the cake, for fear her mother can read her thoughts just by looking at her face.

'Not with me or any of the women in our family. Babies pop out nine months after the wedding night. Once is all it takes.'

'Maybe there's something wrong with me. Maybe the magic ran out.' Effie shrugs. Her mother grabs her arm, and she looks up at her.

'We're safe here. Do you want to know how hard it is out there? Do you want to be homeless? Starving? Sick? Hurt?' She squeezes her arm so tight that Effie fears it will bruise and she'll have to lie to Charlie about it.

'No, Mama.' She can't get breath behind her words and they come out barely above a whisper.

'If he doesn't manage his husbandly duties by the end of the year, he's gone. We don't have the time to waste.' When she lets go, Effie grabs the table to keep from falling.

'That's only two months from now!' Her eyes are wet. She's not sure if she's crying from the pain or the panic.

'Then you'd best get to work, girl.'

Their baby girl is born into an especially muggy July night after 30 hours of labor. Effie weeps at the sight of her, and Charlie and Wanetta do most of the caring. All Effie concedes to is nursing. She spends the time watching her tears drop on her daughter's fuzzy little head and wishes Charlie had walked past the farm that day and never entered her life.

When the baby is three weeks old, Charlie says they need to name her. They're in the kitchen and their daughter is upstairs with Wanetta. Effie is weaving dough for the top of a blueberry pie.

'Just pick a name. I don't care.' She pulls too hard and tears one of the strips. 'I'm busy, okay?'

'Effie.' Charlie comes over to her and takes her flour dusted hands in his own. 'Our baby's name isn't what I'm worried about. Are you okay?'

'I'm fine. Breathing. Eating. Sleeping. Trying to make a pie.'

'Why did you suddenly decide… that night?'

'The time had come.'

He lets go of her hands and sighs.

'Do you… not love her?'

She sometimes can't breathe for the love she feels for her little girl. If she hated her, it would be so much easier. She wouldn't be drowning in guilt over bringing her into the only life any child of hers will ever have.

'No. But I worry about what I can offer her.' She tries to extract the torn strip of dough and rips another in the process. Now the whole thing is ruined.

'Every parent worries about that. But we're safe here.'

'What did my mother say?' she asks, terrified at hearing her mother's words coming out of his mouth.

'About what?'

'Nothing.' Effie shakes her head, trying to dislodge the unpleasant thoughts that nestle there. 'What do you want to name her?' She squishes the dough back together to re-roll and start over.

Elspeth, named after her paternal great grandmother, grows fast. Effie soon falls into a routine of showing her affection. It's not hard. Her daughter's huge inquiring eyes seem to want to swallow the world whole and her chubby little hands grasp at everything, but especially her mama. Charlie often expresses pleasure in seeing his "two girls" so happy together. Wanetta praises her daughter for her change in mood.

'The best way is to just give in to it.'

Effie doesn't ask if Wanetta ever loved her like she loves Elspeth.

Charlie finally manages to get the truck fixed and suggests they all go into town after breakfast.

'Let's show off our lovely little girl,' he says, reaching out his finger for Elspeth to grab. She gurgles with laughter as Charlie pulls like he can't get free.

'I don't feel like going into town. Getting all dressed up and my hair… it's just so much work. Maybe another day?' She tries to keep panic out of her voice.

'Well, I'm going today anyway. You need me to pick up anything?' He finally escapes Elspeth's grip and takes the spoon and bowl of applesauce Effie hands him.

'No.' She watches Charlie take a spoonful and guide it to Elspeth's mouth.

Later that day, Effie asks Wanetta how she got her father to stop asking her to go places.

'That man? Didn't ever occur to him I was on the farm all the time. Your Charlie being a problem?'

'Not a problem, no,' Effie says, staring down at the mop as she drags it along the kitchen floor.

Eventually, Charlie stops asking Effie outright about coming into town and starts bringing back gifts. Books. Candy. Ribbons. He reminds her that if she changes her mind, he'll be right with her the whole time. She could pick out her own books. Maybe even join the new public library. But he's put off easily enough with a smile and a kiss. Until Elspeth turns five.

'It's about time we send her to school.'

They are in bed together. Effie sets down her book. She takes a deep breath before answering.

'Is there something wrong with me?'

'Of course not,' Charlie kisses her cheek and puts an arm around her. 'You, my love, are perfect. I know you didn't go to school, but do you ever think that might be why you don't like going into town?'

'What's so good about town?'

'There's an ice cream parlour.'

She laughs and he smiles, gently pulling her into a hug.

'Have I ever mentioned the library? And they've built a new elementary school. I asked the principal if she and the kindergarten teacher would visit us.'

Effie pulls away.

'When?'

'Tomorrow, after lunch.'

'Do I have any say in this?'

'Of course, we will discuss it and decide together after the meeting.'

Effie says nothing.

'Elspeth is as smart as her mother. I know you worry that we can't give her much. An education is one thing we can give her.'

Effie opens her book again. She stares at the page, not seeing it. Charlie turns over so he's facing away from her. Her head is filled with terrible things that will happen if he insists on sending their daughter to school.

Elspeth is immediately smitten with Miss Violet, the kindergarten teacher. She shows off her books while telling her all about the farm and her favourite animals. There are smiles and handshakes and Effie feels like she did on the day her daughter came into the world. She excuses herself to hold onto the kitchen sink and watch her tears hit the well-worn porcelain. She jumps when she feels a hand on her back.

'You need to deal with this, or I will,' Wanetta says. Effie knows well how her mother solves problems. She helped bury the bodies.

'I don't believe you,' says Charlie. He's in bed while Effie sits at her vanity, brushing her hair. She decided the truth is all she can offer.

'Have I ever lied to you?'

'Well, I've never been comfortable with how… insistent you were the night that Elspeth was, you know.'

'Now you know why I was insistent.'

'There's a family blessing that protects the farm but only if the women never leave it?'

'Curse. Mama calls it a blessing, but it's a curse. It's also why we only have Elspeth. One girl a generation. Never two and never any boys. I suppose that's a sort of mercy.'

'If I asked your mother about this?'

'She might admit it. She might also kill you to keep you from taking Elspeth to school. Don't tell me you don't believe that. You've lived here long enough to know she's not… incapable of such a thing.'

'How do you know this isn't something she made up? A lie so you won't leave her all alone?'

'It's a pretty convincing lie. The only place where anything grows for miles is here. When we sell our crops, the price is always more than fair. None of the animals ever get sick. We're never seriously sick or hurt. How is any of that possible without magic?'

'Okay, but where does it come from and how do you know the rules?'

'My great great grandmother. The farm was failing, and they had no money, so she made a bargain.'

'With the devil? Did she go down to the crossroads?' he says it like a joke, but he doesn't laugh. Effie pulls strands of hair from her brush and stuffs them into the hair saver. Charlie comes over and sits on the floor. He settles his head on her lap. She strokes his hair.

'There is something… different about this farm,' he says. 'I never brought it up because questioning my blessings after so many terrible years seemed ungrateful.' He looks up at her and for a moment she sees the sharp cheekbones and shadows from the day he showed up at the farm looking for work. She leans down and kisses him.

'If you tell Mama that you'll forget about Elspeth and school we'll be safe.'

'What about your father? Did he know?'

'He wasn't like you. He didn't care about us.' She doesn't want to speak that truth aloud because she worries her own part in it will make him feel differently about her. She doesn't know why she cares so much. Scaring him off could save his life. But not now, not with Elspeth. Even if Effie managed to make him despise her, he'd never leave their daughter behind.

'I'm sorry.' Charlie takes her hand, and squeezes it.

'It's nothing for you to be sorry about.'

'What happens when you leave?'

'It's over and we face the outside world like everyone else. But my mother will never let us.'

'What if we leave without telling her?'

The next morning, Charlie says they'll wait another year for school.

'Why? You seemed very set on it yesterday,' Wanetta says. She glances at Effie, who quickly turns her attention back to frying eggs.

'Elspeth is small for her age. She'll fit in better with the other kids next year,' is all Charlie says before heading outside.

'Another year?' Wanetta says to Effie. 'And what will you say next year to put him off?'

'I'll figure it out, Mama.' She flips one of the eggs and the yolk breaks. She stares into the orangey yellow puddle and takes shallow breaths. She only agreed to Charlie's plan because it wasn't as dangerous as confronting Wanetta, but she doesn't think she can go through with it.

Effie catches her mom in the barn the next day. She's got the old wooden ladder out and there's a saw on the ground.

'What are you doing?' she asks. But she knows. She did that with the first stranger. He was on the farm for nearly a year. The man was kind as anything and clearly not interested in a sixteen-year-old girl. Effie hinted that he should move on, but Wanetta got to him first. Effie goes over to the ladder and studies the rungs, looking for signs of sawing.

'Do you actually love him?' Wanetta asks.

'I don't have to love someone to not want them to die!'

'People die a lot on farms. Dangerous work.'

'Not on this farm. Not unless you do something.'

'A year will go fast, better figure out something more permanent.'

'Until you do, right?'

Wanetta shrugs and leaves. Effie returns to studying the ladder.

Effie finds nothing wrong with the ladder and doesn't catch Wanetta doing anything else. Still, she worries. She sniffs the sugar bowl before breakfast. She checks ladder rungs and stair steps daily. She hides sharp objects. She searches every room her mother goes into for items in odd places. She tells Charlie he needs to say he's changed his mind about Elspeth going to school.

'I'm not doing that. It's silly. It's also a lie.'

'Lying could save lives,' Effie says.

'Leaving could save lives.'

Effie wants to slap him but bursts into tears instead. Charlie pulls her close and makes soothing noises. He gives her his hanky and tells her it will be okay.

'I thought you weren't going to lie,' she says.

Effie dreams over and over about walking off the farm. Sometimes she dies. Sometimes she finds nothing. The outside world she once stared at longingly just an empty nothingness. Maybe there is no escape. In her worst dreams, it's Elspeth who breaks the spell. She chases a butterfly past the mailbox and disappears.

Such dreams pull her out of sleep. She gets up and goes to Elspeth's room. She needs to make sure she's still there. She watches her little girl's chest rise and fall until she can't keep her eyes open and needs to return to her own bed.

One morning Charlie goes into town to "pick up some things". He comes back an hour later saying the truck broke down and he had it towed to the garage in town. Effie knows the truck is really sitting just outside the property line and packed with everything they'll take with them.

They didn't tell Elspeth for fear of her saying something to Wanetta. Effie is jumpy all day. She's not sure there aren't other consequences for breaking the spell beyond what her mother's told her. She fears her dreams are more than just worries racing around in her head. She didn't tell Charlie about them, but she did make it clear she's crossing alone.

She can't stop feeling guilty about leaving Wanetta by herself to face an uncertain future. It seems far crueler than anything her mother ever did to her. After all, her mother was only ever trying to protect them. She tells herself she has no choice, but that's a lie. She's got a lot of choices; she just doesn't like any of them.

'Mama?'

Effie jumps and drops the mop. She picks it up and leans it against the counter.

'Yes, my lovely?' she looks down at Elspeth. Wispy curls escape her braids and dirt dots her nose.

'I can't find my book.'

Charlie buys even more books for Elspeth than he does for Effie. She chastises him for spoiling her, but he keeps doing it anyway.

'Which one?' Effie asks, using a corner of her apron to wipe her daughter's nose.

'The rabbit one.'

"The rabbit one" is a Beatrix Potter treasury already in the truck. Effie distinctly recalls setting it aside with all the other items Charlie woke up extra early to put in the truck.

'You're always taking books outside. Go and check under the oak tree, okay?' She feels terrible for lying, even if it is nothing compared to all the things she hasn't told her daughter.

'What's going on?' Wanetta asks an hour later. Effie managed to talk Elspeth into reading *Raggedy Ann in Cookie Land*. Now she's sitting under the oak while Effie hangs laundry. She almost drops the sheet in her hands when her mother appears.

'Hanging laundry. Elspeth's reading.'

'That is not what I mean, and you know it. You and Charlie are conspiring.'

'We're married. Aren't we allowed a little privacy?'

Wanetta eyes Elspeth before turning back to her daughter.

'Don't let a man you barely know talk you into doing something stupid.'

'Too late, I already married him,' Effie whispers to herself as she pulls a clothespin out of her apron pocket. She turns to look at Elspeth. Her daughter is distracted from her book by a passing butterfly. She follows its path with interest and delight in her face. Effie feels sick to her stomach.

They leave the house just after midnight, slipping out the kitchen door. Effie carries a sleeping Elspeth in her arms, trying to enjoy what might be her last moments with her. Small as she is, she's still heavy, and halfway down the lane she needs to hand her to Charlie. There's a full moon and the night is bright and warm. They don't speak, as if they fear being overheard. When they reach the mailbox, Effie allows herself a moment of relief before Wanetta steps out of the corn, pointing a rifle at Charlie.

'Mama!' Effie says, stepping in front of her husband and child.

'I knew you were up to no good.'

'Put the gun down. That is your granddaughter!'

Effie walks towards her, looking into her mother's eyes. She presses against the rifle with her chest and reaches out, as if to pull the trigger herself. Wanetta pulls back and the air cracks. Effie looks down at her chest, expecting to see a hole but the faded orange calico is unblemished. She looks back up and sees her mother standing in the road.

Wanetta runs back onto the property, but the crops are already drying and dribbling into dust. When Elspeth looks back, the farmhouse appears long abandoned. The paint is peeling, the front door hangs at an angle and the porch rails are more than half gone. The few remaining windows have jagged cracks in them. Wanetta sinks to the ground, dirt puffing into the air. She lets out a howl that wakes Elspeth. The girl yawns, rubs her eyes, and looks around her.

'Papa? What happened?'

Charlie is staring at the empty field and doesn't seem to have noticed Elspeth's question. Effie steps over the property line herself. The world doesn't disappear and she's still breathing. She goes back and gives her mother a hug. Wanetta is crying and doesn't look at her. Effie goes over and takes her daughter from Charlie's arms.

'Oh, baby,' she says. Elspeth now feels as light as a summer dress or a slice of angel food cake. 'Have I got a bedtime story for you.'

NORA SCHINNERL

THE SKULL PAINTER

It makes a very specific sound to cut through human flesh – or any kind of flesh, I suppose – wet and sucking, as if the muscles don't quite want to be parted from the bones. It horrified me, in the beginning. The way it sounded alive, the way I could interpret feeling into its smacking noises, the way its softness squished under my fingers. The strained toughness of the ligaments. The violence needed to break a bone you can't cut out whole.

Oh, I apologise. This is probably a horrible way to start a letter. I'm not used to writing letters – or talking at all. I guess you noticed, or you'd be as inept at social interactions as I am, which would be strange for a journalist. It's just that I noticed the question in your eyes, the only one you ever held back. It surprised me endlessly that you didn't ask. Maybe it's why I liked you so much. After all, it's the first thing most outsiders want to know — not that they're many — but they all ask the same repetitive questions. How does it feel to cut into human flesh, to remove bones for a funeral? Is it gross? How can you stand doing something so disgusting for a living?

I wonder why you didn't ask. I like to pretend it's because you didn't want to upset me, but that wouldn't make much sense for a journalist, would it?

I arrived at this colony when I was eighteen. I remember this was a question you did ask, one of many I didn't deign to answer. I grew up on an orbiter station. When I was a kid, I wanted to be a pilot. I can almost feel you smirking at this, since half the galaxy has wanted to be a pilot at some point. But I was truly committed, I swear. Sometimes it felt like all I ever did in my youth was stick my nose into one textbook or another. I wasn't particularly good at studying; always had to pore over every sentence, stare at every equation for hours until it stuck in my mind. Then came eleventh grade, second-to-last year, and the Big Ship companies paid a visit to pick favourites for the piloting license. I remember my confusion when they didn't choose any of the most intelligent students, or the fittest, or even the ones with the best social grading. Took me a while to figure out they'd simply picked the richest kids.

It devastated me. I was a Mandatory, no parents, no riches. To realise that no matter how hard I studied, how much I strained my eyes reading textbooks all night… I would never get the chance to travel through space. Not because I was too dumb, but because I had no one handing out bribes in my name. It broke something in me, this realisation. From one day to the next I abandoned every pretence of interest in studying. I didn't fail my exams – narrowly – mostly because failing would have drawn attention and every attention, as far as I was concerned, was suddenly bad. Instead, I drew endless lines and ornaments on the margins of my papers, then erased them all before submitting. I don't think anyone ever noticed.

Ah, do you even know what a Mandatory is? I guess you must have grown up on a planet? Space screws something up in our genes, or maybe in our minds, nobody's quite sure. No real sunlight, no soil, no sky, you get the gist. What that means is a lot less babies are born in space, and orbiter stations – at least the remote ones like the one I grew up on – are constantly on the brink of dying out, so they came up with the Mandatory system. Means every single woman able to get children is required to have two to keep the population stable. They try from when you're twenty to when you're thirty-five, in-vitro fertilisation. Explains why I didn't stick around the station, doesn't it? Men are required to donate sperm and pay extra taxes, as if that would make up for having an unwanted baby.

Mandatories grow up in station care, all the education and facilities provided. Most children around me had birth parents visiting the dorms from time to time, but not me. People told me my birth Mum wasn't on the station any longer. I thought they lied, of course. Kept coming up with reasons why she couldn't visit, plots and secret agents. Kept a lookout every day for someone with the same dust-coloured hair, or the same drawn-in shoulders, all in vain.

I finally stopped looking when I went planetside and left for Rouge. Nothing to look for anymore, nothing but red. All I could see, even when I closed my eyes, for months and months on end, was red. I thought it was all one colour in the beginning. Just red, one word to describe my whole new world. How stupid.

Most splotches of colour you get on Rouge are its people, all their gold and ginger hair and brilliant blue eyes. I fit in with them even less than with the station crowd. People used to tell me I have brunette hair, but I knew them all for liars. Always had dust-coloured hair – station-dust, almost translucent with just a hint of dirty brown. Nowadays, I'm not so sure. Did you do that experiment as well, in school? The one where you scribble with a marker on a piece of coffee filter, put it in liquid and watch the paint separate into reds and blues and yellows? I know it was meant to demonstrate chromatography, but what always struck me most was not that colour separated, but that it traveled at all, that it crept along the paper as if it was contagious. Rouge's dust is like that. It sticks to you, it stains you. The cracks in your fingers first, then your clothes and your cheeks and your teeth until it even seeps into your dust-coloured hair. Or maybe that's just my imagination.

We have red potatoes here, did you know that? Too much iron in the soil, it diffuses into them. Into everything. People tell me the potatoes taste like steak. I wouldn't know, never had steak. We trade them with the mining corporation on our moon, sometimes, for grain and fruit that doesn't taste like blood.

I hated the colour so much. Red. I hated everything. A quiet hate, though. I think I just needed something to hate, then. I mixed my first colour from the orangeish dust so fine it looked like pigment already. I can't remember why, exactly, I did it. I think, deep down, I felt that if everything were red, if the whole planet were swallowed in its maw, the colour would finally be sated and the world would simply end. I think that's why I started painting the bones, with the intention of simply trying to drown everything in colour, of bringing about the end of the world. I still kind of like the sentiment.

You asked me if I was religious. About the only question I actually answered. Yes, I live on a planet classified as a religious colony. No, I don't believe in anything. It was not a requirement. I don't even believe in that end-of-the-world thing I wrote up there, that's merely the kind of delusion you need now and again to appease an angry heart. I go down to their community house, sometimes, while they hold mass, to listen to their voices. You can't make out any words from outside, only the mood of their songs and mumbled replies to prayers. I never go inside.

I just realised I made it sound as if the orbiter station was the worst place ever, as if growing up an orbiter led to all the anger and bitterness that drove me here. It wasn't — at least not exclusively. Not sure I would've turned out differently in any other place. Except for the Mandatory pregnancies, the station treated its citizens quite decently. After graduation, between seventeen and eighteen, all the station kids got half a year off. Just off. For deciding where to go next, officially, what to do with your life, for volunteer projects and extra classes. I pretty much slept through it all, just squandered the whole six months. Stayed up late, slept long, drew invisible squiggles with my fingers on every available surface. I guess I was always prone to drawing when bored. Never with colour, though. I just didn't want any sign of me, any fragment, to last. I didn't go to the parties. Maybe you noticed, I don't like people so much. Most people, anyway.

I had a girlfriend then. Léna. I didn't mention her to you (not that I mentioned much at all) mostly because I didn't want you to get the wrong impression. Stupid. As if it would have mattered. I was a sullen teenager then, and she was the only one who could stand my moods, for a time.

Six months can feel like an eternity, or like no time at all. Or both, I suppose. When the six months are over and you realise you've wasted them all with sleep and boredom, when you're finally considered an adult and handed your assignment choices… Well, if you're clever, or handy, or social, or rich, or *anything*, really, you get a long list to choose from. I got four, which is the minimum requirement. Léna decided she'd stay on the station and work in the Mandatory Nursery… I didn't even know she liked kids! How can you not know something so integral about the only person you ever thought you understood? Maybe I overreacted, I don't know. Maybe I didn't. I ended up with two of my assignments on the station and two on a forlorn colony planet and had no trouble choosing Rouge.

Rouge. Means *red* in an Old Earth language, did you know that? I remember how, at first, I thought it was named after makeup. Kind of funny, thinking a religious dump like Rouge is named after makeup, isn't it?

I wonder if you knew what to expect before you arrived. You must have known you'd be stuck here for months before the next cargo shuttle docked. I wonder what made you want to come. The thrill? The novelty? Your work contract? Or did you simply want to satisfy your curiosity? Did you know what Rouge would look like? The rocks and plains, the soft curves, the way the horizon blends into the sky so you're never ever sure where one ends and the other begins? Did you look up some pretty pictures, beforehand? I'm not even sure if their religion allows pictures to be taken. Their. They. You know who I mean. Strange, isn't it? I've been living here for almost sixteen years and I still haven't come up with a name for the people of Rouge. There's just no need for it. There's me. And there's them.

They live in six villages, just far enough apart for their fields not to overlap. Everything beyond the villages is rock and dunes, red and dust and emptiness. I live alone in my little house, as far away from Koppa as they agreed to build a house for me. I don't know how many people live on Rouge, altogether, three thousand maybe? In a good week I speak with two of them. First one is Esther, the woman handing out weekly food rations. I'm sure you met her, there's no escaping her gossip. Second one is Elijah.

I have no idea why Elijah is still sticking around. Or, well, maybe I do. To be honest, it's quite impressive how well he managed to ignore me ignoring him. Just like you, really. Seems to be the key to making me fond of someone. In the beginning I thought he'd leave after his morbid curiosity was satisfied, like the other pesky children. He was so little then, all freckles and knees and messy hair. I thought the easiest way of getting rid of him was doing nothing. But he kept coming back, kept watching with these big curious eyes he has, until I put a knife in his hands. Guess that makes him my apprentice. If I had to guess, I'd say it's the neatness of our bones that fascinates him, the way everything serves a purpose, everything has its proper place. The meticulousness of it all. He's just that kind of boy.

Sometimes, when I think back, I'm still amazed Rouge let me stay. Doesn't take much in the way of reading people to know that nobody expected me to stick around. Not in the beginning at least, gloomy teenager that I was, all space-slick and coughing up the dust. Some of them even tried pushing me into taking the other job, organising the cargo shuttle. The one they'd labeled communication/accounting. But that would have required something like social skills. Cutting up people requires no skills, except maybe a strong stomach. I went for funeral/recycling.

Do you know how many vertebrae are in the spine? The way they interlock with the hipbone? The fragile breastbone all your ribs are slotted into? The jigsaw puzzle of your palm? The first thing I think about these days when I look at a person is where to position the knife. Just in case, you know? I wonder if you recoil at the thought. I did, in the beginning.

My first corpse took me a whole week. It's messy work, cutting out the bones, if you have no idea what you're doing. I was crying so hard I could barely see. Not out of pity, the corpse was a wiry old man I didn't recognise. I cried out of revulsion; for the way he was all limp in my hands, the way his lips flapped open when I moved him, the way I saw him inside out, all red and raw. For the thought that this was it, for the rest of my life the only people I would know intimately and without fail would be the dead. I remember feeling parched, like paper, for weeks after, my meagre allotted water not able to replenish the tears.

Afterwards, I stood in the shower until my power allowance for the week was gone. They told me that space people don't like the shower much (that's how they refer to me, orbiters, shuttle pilots, journalists: space people), but I always found it soothing. The way the sand pelts you, like it has hands; tiny, stinging, indifferent hands. It sands you down, polishes you, then covers up all the scars, even the invisible ones. As if it adds a layer instead of taking one away: a spacesuit, a suit of armour.

You asked me how it worked. You asked so many questions, I mean, you were worse than Elijah. Their traditions, their reasons, my reasons. Why would I know any of it? I just cut things. Religion is a mystery to me. Sometimes I envy them, you know. The faith they put in their God, their utter conviction that the world is how it should be, that it all makes sense even if they don't understand how. I can see it in their eyes whenever they bring me a corpse, under the dust and the exhaustion.

Did you find out about the death-gifts while you were here? One of the relatives always trudges over a day before they bring the corpse. They used to hang around my door and wait, just standing there, looking at me with their solemn, patient faces. I didn't bother coming out of the house after the first few months and they started leaving their death-gifts on my doorstep: a loaf of bitter bread, or a sack of red potatoes, or a flask of dusty moonshine for my efforts. As if I cut people up as a courtesy, not as a job.

It's always young guys from Koppa carrying the corpse to my house. They never wheeze, like I would have. The gravity on Rouge is the same as on the orbiter stations; the atmosphere, though, is a different brand. A little less oxygen, a little more nitrogen. Leaves you forever short of breath.

First thing I do with the corpse is drain the blood. Do you know how much blood is in a body? It's five litres, give or take. Me and Elijah make a game of guessing the exact number, sometimes, while we wait for it to drip down. Takes about a day. I store the blood in one of these plastic containers you see in the fields, on the dust sleds. That's what they use it for, you know? Watering the fields. Even more iron for the red potatoes. Rouge isn't exactly a welcoming planet, you can't let anything go to waste here. You wash your dishes with dust, you shower in sand, and if you drink, you do so out of a sucking bottle to make sure you never ever spill a drop. That's what the supply shuttle is for, mainly. For ferrying in water. Because it doesn't matter how careful they are, how many moisture collectors they put up, some of it will always leak into the dust and the sand. Sometimes I wonder if one day, after thousands and thousands of years, all our wayward perspiration will combine into a cloud and rain onto our descendants' heads.

It's why, when I mix my colours, I never take the fresh blood. It would be stealing and stealing moisture is as bad as it gets on Rouge. Instead, I scrape off dried flakes from the insides of the emptied tanks. It makes a dark red colour, almost brown, smooth and terrific to paint with.

As soon as the corpse is bled dry, I cut out the bones. I've gotten plenty of practice in the last sixteen years, so it barely takes me a day now before I chuck the bones into a pot to salvage the marrow. When I'm done, nothing but the bones remain. I've gotten pretty good at fitting a whole skeleton into a shipment crate by now. A whole person, or at least what's left of a person after you take away all the nutritious bits.

You asked me why they do it, of course. Why they bother. Religion, I guess? Maybe you can come up with a better reason to pour all those resources into a stupid, antiquated belief system, I'm sure I can't. What I can tell you is that Rouge is greedy. There's no water, no bacteria, no fertile soil to be had. Rouge sucks up all the life, all the nutrition we can give it. We feed it with blood and flesh and waste, with marrow and gristle, with hair and skin, and all it gives us are small hard potatoes, stringy turnips and wilting kale. But it doesn't need the calcium, plenty enough in the rocks as it is. The bones are all the colony can spare. I don't know who came up with the half-witted idea of sending the bones to be buried on Old Earth. It takes two hundred years to reach it from here, two hundred years until their skeletons will be dumped in fertile soil just so they can pretend to one day awaken in an imaginary paradise. I wonder if it ever occurred to them that along the way some pilot might cut corners and dump the bones into the atmosphere of a random planet. Probably not. That's faith for you.

There's not much in the way of news to be had here; the supply shuttle is the only off-planet communication we have. Months outdated, of course. I wonder how you coped with that, being a journalist. Anyway, what I wanted to say is, when I became famous I didn't realise it for almost a year. I still don't know what happened, exactly. An accident? Customs control? Maybe I should have asked you for details. Nobody was supposed to open the crates before they reached Old Earth, two hundred years from now and with me long beyond caring. But somebody must have, because one day the cargo shuttle arrived carrying a magazine with my paintings covering the front page – and on the next shuttle there you were.

You probably know every detail of how people discovered it, the way it spread, all the little twists and turns. Why else would they have sent you? You'll probably laugh at my lack of information, my naivety. But here's what I know anyway: somehow, someone opened the crates and discovered the patterns I had drawn on the bones, years and years of swirls and lines and dots. This someone thought it would be a marvellous idea to inform the religious authorities. From what I know, they wanted to sue me quietly. I have no idea what they expected to get out of suing me. I mean, Rouge pays me in food and water and the morsel of station money I get is enough for me to buy the occasional secondhand book from the supply shuttle and that's it. Welcome to the outer systems. But before they could even locate me, a militant atheist group stepped in and started raising hell. Creepy people who like painted bones got wind of it, then newspeople who like to write about creepy people, then artists who pounce at anything strange, then art collectors with too much money to spend. Before I even knew somebody wanted to sue me, I had lawyers working for me who cost more than all the water Rouge imports in a year. Earth is strange. I guess they're still bickering about me in some court or other.

Did you know some people offered me millions to buy the bones? They're not mine, didn't they notice? I didn't even paint them to be Art, or a statement, or to make a point or any of the other reasons they credited me with. I got bored, that's all. Rouge is religious, not fanatic; they have things like vaccinations and penicillin. Three thousand people with acceptable healthcare leaves me with loads of time on my hands, and the stash of paperback novels Koppa keeps in their community building is not especially large.

Did you know some people from nearby stations tried sending me paint for a while? Green and yellow and blue. What would I do with green paint? Nothing here is green, green wouldn't be appropriate. I use an orange-tinged red made from dust. I use a brownish red made from blood. And I use white made out of ground bones, never quite pure because I can't keep the dust out of the jar. I bind the pigments with oil out of my food supply. My first brushes were constructed out of tufts of my own hair and they still work, so why should I change them? I guess I could order actual supplies, now that I don't have to act in secrecy anymore, but it would feel weird.

Did you read the articles they wrote about me? All the names they came up with? I liked Bone Artist best, I think. Don't know why Skull Painter stuck. I don't even like to paint skulls, they're so definite. You can't make a skull look like anything else but a skull; eye sockets are always eye sockets, teeth always recognisable as teeth. Give me long bones, humeri and femora. You can paint stories on long bones, winding around and around and around. Or shoulder blades. You can put a whole world on a shoulder blade.

I had no idea how the people of Rouge would take it, my fame. Me desecrating the bones they spent so much time and effort on ferrying away. For religious people, they're remarkably discreet. I mean, you've met them. They're simply impossible to predict. After I saw that picture on the front page of the magazine… I froze. I didn't know what to do. Maybe I panicked a little. If I had seen it, who else had? Or rather, who hadn't? Worry like this is a disease, makes you queasy and lightheaded whenever you feel somebody's eyes on you. I can't actually remember how I spent those days, just that I had this one repetitive thought stuck in my head. What would I do if they made me leave? I still don't know the answer.

Nobody mentioned a thing, of course. Spend enough time here and you'll find out that's just how Rouge works. When the dreaded knock on my door came, it wasn't the angry mob of farmers I had expected. Instead, there was this little girl carrying a death-gift. Red potato cake. I didn't know what to make of it, so, like always, I kept my door shut and waited for her to go away. She wouldn't, though. Just stood there, knocking from time to time. They all seem to have it, this infuriating Rouge patience. I don't know if it comes with the genes or with the religion. When I finally opened the door, she asked me to paint an elephant for her grandma. She must have seen one in the old picture books they keep in the schoolhouse; I had to go and check what an elephant even looked like. And that was it. That was all. Apparently this is how new traditions are born.

Nowadays, none of them leave silently. They stick around, wait until I open the door to take their death-gifts and then recite their painting requests. Stars, mountains, dots, waves, potatoes. They always tell me in station language as well. It's not as if I couldn't understand theirs after sixteen years on Rouge, even if they still tease me about having the stars in my voice. I don't know, maybe they want to be sure. They never get to see it, you know. I could write insults or scatter the bones or not do anything at all and they would never know. Rouge and their stupid faith. Of course I paint exactly what they ask me to.

Elijah started watching me recently. He just lingered after the bones were done, so I showed him how to mix the paint. He's good at it, too. I wonder how he would paint, if it would be the same swirly strokes I make, or if it would be intricate geometric things, or abstract blobs, or painstakingly realistic drawings. I guess it says something about your soul, the way you paint.

I'll never know. Even if one day I hand him a batch of bones and a palette, they will be his alone; I wouldn't peek. The bones are made for secrecy. It's not the paintings that make them special, no matter how good people might claim they are – it's the way nobody will ever know. So no, I don't feel bad about no one ever getting to admire my art (except for the bit that's already leaked). I remember it was the answer I felt you'd have the most trouble with understanding. My paintings are made to stay hidden. It's what makes them special. It's their point.

You probably wonder why I wrote you all this, this long letter, when I never answered anything while you stayed on Rouge, trudging up to my house in your too-bright space clothes, with this too-bright curiosity of yours. Truth is, I thought if I answered you'd stop coming. That if I just kept not answering, not showing any reaction, you'd always have to come back. That the mystery would intrigue you in a way answers never could. You left anyway, of course, but still I wonder. You never stopped asking questions. I remember your last one just as well as the first.

Pretend that I wanted all my fame, pretend that I agreed to paint rich people's bones and draw murals on desolate station walls, pretend that I would accompany you to make my fortune. What would I do with said fortune? I didn't reply, then. I didn't know what to say. I've never before had the possibility of a fortune to spend. But the question stuck in my mind and by now I've come up with an answer. I'm not sure it will satisfy your readers, though. I'll tell you anyway, and you can proceed with this truth however you like. It's yours, my last and only gift to you.

If I was a grand artist, renowned throughout the galaxy, I'd spend my fortune drowning my flat in red dust.

AMANDA M. BLAKE

INFILTRATION

I smelled it first, tasted it in each inhale, like a roll of pennies over my tongue – not unpleasant but certainly not something I wanted to swallow. I wrinkled my face and kept bringing the tea to my nose to block out the metal.

I'd never had rooibos tea before the retreat, but Anna, host of a modest row of beachfront shacks, made it every morning after breakfast and every afternoon after lunch and didn't mind sharing.

After trying to make some headway on my novel through the smell, I climbed barefoot down the driftwood steps to the rocky sand. There was the risk of splinters and sharp rocks, the occasional blob of stranded jellyfish, but the experience of sand and stone on sole entranced me as much as the hypnotic rhythm of the rolling waves.

I squinted, then blocked the glare with my hand and tried to discern what of the red was from afterburn and what was the sea.

'Algae bloom.' Anna joined me on the shore, wind-chafed and Viking with her thick cord braid, retired light keeper in boots and cable-knit sweater, working jeans from the men's section, palms as red as her cheeks. 'Red tide. Snuck in unexpected, late advisory. Toxic. Some people are more sensitive to it — headaches, nausea, difficulty breathing, strange dreams. If you're concerned, you can find a room further inland. Or return home.'

I lifted my face to the invisible spray off the sea, which created friction in my hair when I scrubbed it under soft water. The salt gradually coated everything if Anna didn't regularly scrub it down.

I'd planned and budgeted for three weeks of a seaside writing retreat in one of Anna's shacks. Full-sized bed, lumpy chaise longue, plastic breakfast table, electric kettle and drip coffee maker, small stove and fridge for meals, although Anna had invited me to dinner after sunset most nights. Falling asleep to the smell of sea salt and the steady beat of the ocean through open windows. The shacks looked like a strong breeze would topple them like sandcastles, but all I'd had to do during the last storm was close the windows and latch the shutters. The earth had shuddered more than the little house, and Anna had made hot chocolate with the electric kettle.

Most chilly mornings I would walk my word processor to the tea shop in town for a ham and Swiss croissant and English breakfast tea. I picked up groceries from the lethargic general store. I'd set up an out-of-office email message and mostly left my phone on the kitchen counter to pretend it didn't exist, either.

This last week and a half had been the kind of life I'd always imagined, wished for, prayed for. If I thought too much about the end, my heart hurt and words moved like earthworms across summer pavement.

I crossed my arms against the damp that accompanied sunset, when Anna's knitwear started making more sense. 'I have another week and a half booked.'

Anna didn't look at me, but she rarely did. After I knocked on her door upon arrival, I assumed she rented out the shacks from financial desperation and that she hated me for disturbing her peace. She could have slapped my face with a fish the first time she invited me to dinner.

'Grilled cheese with tomato basil tonight,' she said. 'We'll eat inside. Sleep with the windows closed and shutters latched.'

I awoke in a hot sweat, blankets kicked off despite the mosquito whir of the fan.

I climbed out of bed in long sleeves and no pants and lifted open the windows, pushed out the shutters. The moon winked silver between thin scuds of clouds. I stood there for I don't know how long, gripping the wet windowsill, listening to the waves and the interruption of chimes.

Most of the shacks were sparsely decorated – secondhand and second life, faded from time and elements – but although Anna said little, her porch wind chimes of metal, wood, bone, and nutshell sang almost constantly. If the waves were heartbeat and the tide circadian rhythm, the wind chimes were the sea's whispers, through which Anna felt no need to get a word in edgewise.

The sea was talking tonight, and in the distance, a foghorn wailed what my eyes could already see – a blanket swimming in over tide, glowing red between sky and sea.

My stomach roiled with an inexplicable sense of arrival or of someone already arrived, premonitory dread like the anticipation of travel, although I was here and not soon home. Yet, rooted, tasting a whole wrap of pennies in my closing throat, I watched the front and the tide and listened to the distress of chimes.

When the fog hit the shore and swallowed the shacks, pouring into my window, I couldn't see Anna's home anymore, and the chimes seemed distant, stifled, or maybe that was just my ears.

I stirred when dawn inked the dark on the other side of the fog. I was on the floor and not sure why or when I'd fallen. The clouds that had invaded the shack had since evaporated or eddied out the way they'd come.

I sat up. The headache swayed a beat behind, pounding at my skull for patience, but it was the red cast to the room that confused me. I'd awoken to sunrise over the last week and a half; the warm hues hadn't been half this red.

As I climbed to my feet, I noticed smears along my skin. The red wasn't in the light. It coated everything in the finest dew, but on certain materials it coalesced into larger droplets. My shirt, the sheets, the sofa were a subtle pink, but red liquid bled from every pore in the wood and my flesh.

Guilt, because Anna had warned me to shut my windows, but also bewilderment, because I couldn't remember opening them – just the lighthouse moon and the red rolling fog.

Outside, the sand had witnessed a silent massacre. Red pooled on the stones and driftwood and stained the foam. The clear sky above the horizon seemed all the more blue against the dire red that spanned the stretch of sea in my view.

Not sure where to begin and nowhere to go where I didn't leave footprints, I went to the fridge – bloody handprint on the handle. The inside was too bright for my headache but untouched by red until I grabbed one of the bottled waters Anna provided, because tap wasn't always the best tasting here. I drank the entire bottle, grimacing against the cold and clear.

My carpetbag suitcase had absorbed some red, but the interior was waterproof. I stripped off my shirt, wiping off as much as I could, then took some clothes to the bathroom, which had remained largely untouched by the fog, since the door had been closed. I changed into long shorts and a light sweatshirt. No shoes. No escaping the red on the floors and the ground.

The whole line of shacks had been rained with blood. Nestled in concavities were lumps of crimson gel like jellyfish, although too far inland from high tide for that. They shivered even with my gentle footsteps.

I tiptoed through the red-dewed grass and silty, red-streaked soil to Anna's shack, but I couldn't put a foot down without sinking into red, so by the time I reached the porch, I stopped being delicate.

Anna, too, had slept with the windows open. She shivered in scarlet-soaked sheets.

Usually, she woke before dawn. She'd said could feel sunrise in her bones.

I'd never understood that phrase before, but now I felt each individual bone, the very knuckles of my toes. I struggled with the doorknob.

As soon as I managed to get the door open, I staggered to Anna's bed and shook her by the shoulders. She clenched her eyes shut tighter and moaned like a little girl in a nightmare. She wouldn't wake.

I was wondering if it would take too long for an ambulance to come all the way out here, but then Anna finally stirred as though fighting through a forest of spider-floss, fluttering eyelids over eyes as vivid blue and striking as the sky against the beading of red.

'What time is it?' she asked blearily.

I checked the clock on the microwave. 'Nine.'

Anna jerked up, but a headache of her own left her briefly paralysed. When it subsided enough for her to open her eyes again, she looked around in intensifying silence.

'I think the red tide came in on the fog,' I said.

Anna tucked her stained sheets over her front. The fog had soaked the thin shirt into a ghost, exposing her dark nipples and the suggestion of a tattoo over her hip. Her face was bloodless, but her cheeks managed to find a reserve, although she showed no other sign of embarrassment.

'No, Patrice. It doesn't do that.'

Anna gazed over her shoreline as though it were another landscape entirely. My heart jolted off-rhythm from chest to fingertips. When Anna took my hand to lead me from the beach to the paved street, I held her harder.

The salty seafoam breeze pulled at my hair, loose, although Anna had replaited hers. The pebbly surface of the pavement gleamed as though with oil spill, but what filled the cracks and potholes like new rain ran red.

The town, such as it was, was mostly in Cape Cod cool greys and blues, worn as an old boardwalk, but as we entered, the walls were bleeding. Cars and windows dripped plague condensation, and nothing else living walked the street with us. Every sign said CLOSED except the tiny church, which read NOTHING BUT THE BLOOD OF JESUS. If it hadn't been there for the whole week and a half of my retreat, I would have thought it was a bad joke.

'We should go home,' Anna said.

'Maybe someone needs help.'

She stared intently at the tea shop, where I'd drunk gallons of English breakfast tea and crossed the channel for baskets of croissants. I peered through the scum-scrimmed window. I thought I saw the elderly owner, with her nineties floral dresses to match her tea sets, reclining in a spindly parlour chair, her permed hair in disarray and her mouth open as far as the jaw could go and perhaps farther, like deep-sea beasts in the dark.

The mouth closed. Something sprayed the window inside.

'We should go home,' Anna repeated.

Before, Anna had no trouble cycling a small trailer up to town, then loading and hauling what she'd ordered back several times a week. She cleaned the interiors and exteriors of the shacks by herself, fished the ocean in her rubber coveralls. Grey shot through the cornsilk of her hair, and salt and sun had done a number on her skin, but she was a strong woman, with large hands, teeth that could crack crab legs, fists to crack walnuts.

Although I was not as working-fit, I trained for and ran marathons, and I had been doing free weights at home for years.

Yet, exhausted, we dangled our legs over the edge of the bridge. We clung to the railing as though in fear of slipping over onto the surf-struck black rocks below. Cold spray dampened our skin and clothes.

'We should call someone when we get back,' I said.

'There's no one to call,' Anna replied, thin-lipped.

'CDC? NOAA?'

'I'm not confident they would even come. They already warned us of red tide. The rest is the hysterics of small-town yokels who don't know their boots from their behinds. And if it is something, better it lives and dies here, where no one has to know.'

'It's a whole town. Someone has to do something. There are people here.'

'It's off-season. The money went back home. Town might as well be abandoned.'

I thought she was being cynical, but maybe, despite everything I'd gone through in my very different life, I was still a romantic. 'What do you think it is?'

'I think it's not red tide.' She held up her hand for me to help her to her feet.

She didn't let go once we were walking, under the auspices of our collective weakness. The connection made me feel stronger. I hoped it did the same for her.

Back at the shacks, I broke away to run to mine, trying to avoid the gelatine sunning on sand and rock like dissolved sea urchins – larger now, and with a denseness to their centre, although they still jiggled from my seismic footsteps. They also lurched in my direction if my foot came too close.

Red tide was algae. Like toxic mould, it didn't have a will, just a way. It wouldn't behave like this.

The ocean, too, seemed to be thickening, an abattoir soup churning to stew. Clots rode the waves or scattered in the swash that carried in the new rising red tide.

What would it leave behind when it went back out?

Each step up to the porch, my joints threatened to pop blisters of synovial fluid. When I reached the kitchen counter where my phone sat charging, I almost fell to my knees, but I was afraid I wouldn't be able to get up again, so I leaned over the counter instead – the suburban housewife that I used to be, waiting for insistent hands, tolerated to keep him hungry and me fed, yet hungrier.

My cheek still on the vinyl, I unplugged my phone. No matter what button I pushed, it wouldn't turn on.

Red liquid, like bloody tears, dripped from the USB port and the crack on the screen.

I threw the phone on the ground.

Anna didn't ask if I'd had any luck calling anyone. She just brushed the worst of the red off the step where she'd settled and braced me as I sat next to her, no phone, no computer. That had turned on, but the wireless was out.

'I feel sick,' I said. 'And old.'

Maybe fifteen minutes later, as if she'd only just registered my words, she replied, 'You don't look sick.' She intertwined our fingers and rested her head on my shoulder, because she couldn't hold hers up any longer without help. 'Or old.'

Even as my butt went numb on the driftwood step, I couldn't move until the sun was too high in the sky, its glare burning my sensitive eyes. The ache in my bones and muscles deepened like spikes, and the thick coppery smell became unbearable, mingled with decay as thousands and thousands of fish went red-slick belly-up in the receding water. Those still living gasped behind on the beach, along with new clusters of diseased jellyfish or whatever it was that lingered and bloomed on shore.

'We should sleep in another shack tonight,' Anna said. 'Bad red tide or something else, our shacks are contaminated. We air out one of the others, wash all this off of ourselves. Wait it out.'

We shuffled like old wives to gather salvage from the shacks, blood-strewn shipwrecks still bleeding from the walls, dripping from sodden sheets and sofa skirts. My computer and word processor were safe in their storage bags, but I shut them into the kitchen cabinet anyway for additional protection. I couldn't think about my book, although it would have been a nice distraction.

My hands were arthritic claws that struggled with the cap before I swigged more clean water, then gathered the rest of the bottles to burden a bag, along with crackers, and the charcuterie fixings as well as fruit I'd stored in the fridge. Those in the fruit bowl rotted, with a film of gelatinous red instead of mould. I was as eager to eat the uncontaminated food as the rotten. At least the water was refreshing, although it sloshed in my stomach like bathwater in a quake.

It took us ungodly time to reach the third shack and for Anna to fumble with her master keyring to open it. The air inside was that of a swamp crypt, wet and dark and tainted, but when she flipped on the light, it looked dry and grey as kindling. Anna switched on the fan to refresh the dank-dust air.

I relieved her laden shoulders as though I were the strong one, then we shuffled to the bathroom together. I helped her strip her clothes away and reached in to turn on the shower. I feared that if I helped her lay down in the ancient clawfoot tub, she might pull me over on top of her and neither of us would ever move again.

The way she lowered her eyes in shame – not at being seen, but at being seen like this – and rested her head briefly on my shoulder again before stepping into the tub, such an end didn't seem so unpleasant.

Just turn on the water, and when the tub is full, open the drain – constant flow, constant ebb, like the waves, the waves, the waves, rocking, rocking, her powerful body and slowly softening skin, rocking, rocking, rocking…

I turned on the shower.

She stepped under while the water was still cold, with barely a shiver. She smiled a little, all the way to her eyes. 'It's off-season for tourists, Patrice, not me. I'm a woman of the sea. Light keeper all year. Sometimes the hot-water heater doesn't work the way it should, or at all.'

The spray pounded what stain remained on her skin and splattered faded red on the white enamel. After a deep breath, she turned her face into the spray and didn't let it out for a long time. But she did eventually, so I closed the curtain all the way, even as she didn't ask.

I used the toilet, then went to the sink. Washing my hands, I left spatters of red on the enamel there as well. I scrubbed and scrubbed with the soap bar, but the staining never stopped, and when I withdrew my hands, it continued still.

I adjusted the faucet so that the flow was gentler, the line of water clear enough to tell that it wasn't clear at all.

I let Anna have the peaceful beat of rain on her frailer flesh, warm enough to steam the room.

Droplets on the mirror, fine at first, gathered into beads that dripped a deep red.

She came out of the bathroom naked, slow but steadier, strengthened by water and warmth, by inevitability. She went to the windows and opened the glass, unlatched the shutters to swing them wide. Exquisite view from a shabby little shack –

the best-kept secret on the coast for the price, even in a town without a single lobster roll to its name.

As I stood from the sofa without protest, I left a red stain on the thrift cushion. The red had already infiltrated the room. We carried it with us, beading from our pores, falling in our tears, burning through our muscles, grinding our joints with sand to make us pearls.

At the window, the slow strobe of moonlight stunned me. I hadn't realised how late it was, how slow we'd become, but that became less important when Anna held her hand up to fresher air, cool against the stuffiness, sweet with bloody copper and sickly with rot. Sea spray gathered in her palm lines like ink.

'There's nowhere to go,' she said. 'It's in the sea, and the sea is in the air.'

I joined her at the window and held up my arm, where pin-prick ink of my own had gathered, even after attempting to wash it off over and over and over in the kitchen sink. 'In the freshwater, too. In *us*.'

We looked back out on that million-dollar view – now an alien terrain of red, red, red, red beneath a silvered sky. Red tide, red foam, red pools, red gel blooming from other droplets and small puddles into bigger drops, bigger puddles, shudder-ing in rhythm to the pounding waves like the ponderous foot-steps of a deepwater monster.

The red tide was thick now, dead fish stippling to the horizon – or maybe they weren't dead, because those I had thought dead on shore still gasped air that should have killed them hours before. And crawled, crawled up the beach like distant ancestors.

'What is it?' I asked.

Anna smeared the red over my arm with her palm, leaving handprints, fingerprints, shivers. 'I don't know.'

I was the one gasping as she took my face between her rough working hands and pressed her lips to mine. She looked like lipstick had smeared over her mouth when she pulled away. Blood between her teeth, red, red, red tongue, flushed cheeks, whites of her eyes swimming with burst blood vessels.

I hooked my arms under hers, reeled her in as we manoeuvred our groaning bodies to the uncovered mattress. Anna threw a musty quilt on the scratch, I removed my clothes so that we were unashamed together, and we sank and squished onto the bed.

'Of the many I've wanted to forget, you're who I would want to spend last breaths in my moonlight, on my beach.' Anna stroked my face, gathering red on her fingertips. She insinuated her knee between my legs and pressed her thigh at the apex. 'Do you feel it? How it wants to combine? Coalesce?'

'Coagulate,' I finished for her, rocking, rocking like the water, in and out, ebb and flow.

She joined me in the rhythm — first our own, then even I could tell we moved with the red, red sea, each breaking wave a roar, but it was so hard to stop, and we didn't want to. Nerve branches that I'd thought had died between the divorce and the change had just been dormant, alive and swaying now, with the million stars around a mirror-ball moon.

I undid her braid, the silver-shot cornsilk more and more ginger with each pass of my hand combing through. My other hand couldn't seem to move away from the siren of her skin, kneading into the flexing muscle, into flesh, *into.*

Anna was breathless, panting, eyes full red like blood on the moon after an eclipse. She was close, one hand caught on, in, on my head, the other grasping my leg to tuck it into her hip. She shook her head, moaning higher, higher, quivering like the puddles on the beach.

'Is it just the red in you that calls to the red in me?' she asked. Forehead to forehead, her thoughts were mine, and I understood that she begged, pleaded, dared to hope. Behind careful curation, she held galaxies; perhaps she was calmed by the quieter spirals in mine.

We'd been comfortable, comfortable as long-time lovers, comfortable as forever friends, comfortable in her silence and in my occasional chattiness, comfortable in her gruff coolness and my ennui. When she'd taken my hand, it had been the most natural thing in a world gone to red.

'If you had kissed me five days ago, I would have kissed you back.'

She kissed me now, lips to lips, tongue to tongue, interlocked, overlapped, sinking, sinking into each other, weak but rocking still, making our own waves in the soaked-through quilt, weeping, bleeding, pennies between our teeth, on our tongue, swallowed, subsumed, coalesced, coagulated. And yes, we gasped, and yes, we came, and yes, the Venn diagram of us was highlighted red, spreading and spreading in a gelatinous pool, and yes, we forgot, but at least we were we and we had a view, panoramic, and oh, so red.

COREY FARRENKOPF

DRINKERS

The hotel is a chain. There's at least one in every major city. They don't have a pool, or a gym, or the overpriced stores you see in Marriotts and Hotel Sixs. They are short, three or four stories, cement and glass and steel. Inside, the lobby is bathed in a calming light, the carpet reminiscent of a still pool of water, ceilings high overhead. A number of tired looking men and women sit in plush chairs along the room's outskirts, seemingly in a daze, heads nodding, half asleep. Most have bandages covering their right ear, but some have gauze wrapped around their left. I walk between them, as if down a church corridor, the central aisle of a modern cathedral, a song only I can hear playing in my head.

I have the required paper in hand, memories clearly written between blue lines.

Seth.

His name is in almost every sentence.

'Do you have a reservation?' the concierge asks when I reach the front desk, tapping a finger on a tablet.

'It's under Butler,' I reply.

The concierge scrolls.

'Jared?' he asks.

'Jared,' I confirm.

'Good, good. Just need you to fill out the waivers and then I can get you your room key,' the man says, unearthing a pile of documents from inside the desk. There has to be a hundred lines that require my signature. I fold page after page, hastily jotting my name, over and over. I want to be as quick as possible. I don't want to know what I'm signing away.

Halfway through the pile, a rustling noise, fabric on fabric, jostles behind me. I look over my shoulder. A woman is eased from one of the chairs, escorted by the doorman to a cab waiting by the curb. She stumbles. He catches her weight, steering her out into the night.

'She'll certainly be fine,' the concierge says, reassurance not so reassuring.

'I never had a single worry,' I lie.

'Good. A few more signatures and you'll be all set.'

My key is to room 314. I press the card to the automated lock and a slight wheeze emanates from the device, followed by a resonant click. I step from the hall into the room. There is no privacy sign to hang on the door handle, no lock on the door. A pinprick of gooseflesh shakes across my arms. I tell myself it is one night. One night to heal everything.

Seth's been dead for five years. It was the loneliness, the disconnect, present life unable to meet past expectations. I don't have the loneliness, but the rest, it's all there. Hence the hotel. Hence the signatures.

We were in a straight-edge band for a while, then we weren't. Then we were in a melodic hardcore band, and then we weren't. Then we were in a skate punk band, and then we weren't. The group morphed as we aged, playing faster, then slower, then dirgelike. Fans came and went, resonating with one sound, but drifting from another. We couldn't fault them. It was the music we had to make. You don't really get to pick the creative path you take. The path is just there — whether you walk it or not, that's up to you.

But Seth was always walking the path, could never get off it if I'm being honest.

Touring was expensive.

Payouts from streaming services were negligible.

The second jobs that actually paid the bills were too consuming to keep the band together any longer.

So the tours stopped and the records stopped and the fans found other bands to give their listening time to.

Second jobs became the first jobs they truly were, the only jobs. The rest of us started families. I've got two kids, a wife at home waiting for my stay to be over. Our drummer had triplets.

Seth had a cat.

He'd send me videos of him singing new songs to the little tabby, belting anthems with the acoustic guitar he'd had since we were in high school. The cat would nod along to the song. So would I. I don't think he ever recorded any of them. I should put the videos up on the internet, convert the audio into a posthumous CD, but I can't bring myself to do it. That would make them eternal, the songs playing in other ears, life given to the undead with a click of the mouse.

Those songs, they keep playing in my head as if Seth were standing at the end of my bed, guitar in hand, strumming through the night. He followed me to work at the graphic design studio, he sang to me beside the pool at my son's swimming practice. Everywhere I went, the memory of my friend followed, the songs never abating. Over the last three months, his thought-summoned apparition joined the solo act, the shimmering doppelgänger of my long buried best friend visible at each private concert. At first, the hallucination was a welcome encounter, a brother returned from the other side, a reminder of the joy we once shared. But he is incessant. I'm never alone.

Nostalgia truly is a sickness of the past.

That's why his name is on the piece of paper, why all the memories I hope to expunge are focused on him.

Seth has to go.

I don't drink the tea the hotel left on the bedside table, the blue liquid unnatural, though they swear the brew is all organic herbs. I want to forget, but I want to remember, but I want to forget. I raise the porcelain cup to my lips, but can't tip it back. Once something is gone, truly gone, you can never get it back. So there the drink sits, still surface placid, ocean-like in miniature. There isn't much time left for the anaesthetic to take effect. If I want the following scene to be painless, the clock is ticking by, second by second.

Seth is there, haunting the doorway to the bathroom, palm muting power chords over raspy lyrics.

The song sounds like the title track of our first album, the one they played on the radio in the nineties for a day or two. Our agent said they almost added that song to the second Tony Hawk video game, but that fell through. Inclusion could have kept our touring life alive for years, nostalgia alone filling small venues on weeknights.

There's a room in your heart
And a room in your soul
A room in the night
You will never let go

I ask him what the hell the lyrics mean, but he never stops playing. He's little more than a constant hologram projected from somewhere deep inside my skull. Of course he can't answer.

Do you know what it's like to go days without sleep?

Do you know how hard it is to keep a marriage together when madness clings to your throat?

I couldn't save Seth. There was nothing I could do. Everyone else moved on. It wasn't my fault he couldn't. Even if I hadn't ignored those last texts, those late night voice messages. We weren't getting the band back together. I needed to save for my kids' college fund. I needed to keep up with mortgage payments. He was the one with unrealistic expectations, not me. Drop everything and unearth the old van from the scrap lot behind his house? He sounded unhinged. The request was selfish, unkind. Yes, he was right. Nothing brought me the same joy as playing live, a handful of sweaty twenty-some-things screaming our lyrics in the front row, but life moves on. There was no choice of going back, no matter how much I wanted to. Joy only lasts until it doesn't. Seth never understood. He needed the constant flow, the endless drip. Reality was never on his side.

But nearly thirty years of friendship?

That's a lot to feed to the void.

The creature doesn't knock. They expect me to be unconscious, the dreamworld trapped in the cup pulling my eyelids shut. But I couldn't drink the blue liquid, couldn't hammer the last nail into the coffin. I lay on the bed, pressing myself back into the headboard, parting pillows, trying to get as far away from the creature as I can, despite all the research I've done, despite knowing their arrival was what I was paying for, what everyone paid for when they stayed at these hotels.

Their black cloak drifts down to the floor, folds like a streaming shadow around their lithe sexless body. Their face is narrow, skin chalky, eyes two bottomless holes carved from flesh, limbs longer than my own, mouth a tiny line with no lips to speak of. But their face isn't what I flee. No, what makes me recoil is that extra digit drooping off their hands, a sixth finger like a long boneless proboscis. The end is open in a second tapering mouth, no teeth, just inner endless darkness.

Some people call them Thought Vampires.

Others, Drinkers.

The hotels are their homes. So many distraught people require their services. So many can't live with the accumulation of sadness festering in their lives. Seth's suicide is minor compared to what others in the lobby have offered to nourish the creatures.

'The tea,' the Drinker says, gesturing towards the cup on my nightstand.

'Couldn't do it,' I reply.

'I can leave,' the Drinker says. 'No refund, but memories still.'

'No, I don't think that's an option.'

The Drinker nods and moves to the end of the bed, Seth still standing there in the bathroom doorway, playing the same song on repeat.

'You wish to feel?' the Drinker asks, raising their tentacle-like proboscis. The prehensile limb drapes over the comforter, pale flesh made somehow paler by the white fabric.

'I do,' I reply, the words coming out though I hadn't known they would.

'The paper,' the creature says.

I lift the scrap from my bedside table, reading over the memories one last time:

The entire first tour, Seth in the driver's seat.

The makeshift studio we built in his stepdad's garage.

The hospital trip we'd taken after a stagediver knocked him headlong into the guitar amp.

The Warped Tour stint.

The flea market where we found his first Gibson.

The Chinese buffet after signing our first record deal.

The time he played a grunge version of Baby Shark at my son's birthday party.

There is so much more on the list, but something is missing, so I jot a final line, not caring what of my contemporary life gets swallowed along with it:

Every night he leaned in my bedroom, playing his songs. The repetition. The repetition.

'It is honourable to watch them go,' the Drinker says, sliding close to me across the bed, like a dorm-room lover confident about the act to follow. They stop a foot away, depressing the mattress, feet on the floor, robes pooling, proboscis stretching between us. 'Please give.'

I hand over the paper.

They read each line.

'All?' it asks.

'All,' I reply.

The Drinker nods, gives me what I imagine they imagine is a reassuring smile, and raises their free hand. Then the proboscis is in my ear, sliding deeper and deeper. The appendage writhes through fleshy channels, worming about my brain, grooves like well-trodden paths, searching, prowling, delving. The pain is slight. I grip the headboard with white knuckles. Just discomfort, the alien sensation turning my stomach, an internal wetness against an internal wetness that shouldn't be there. Then the appendage stops, hunt halted. The Drinker begins to hum. The hum is almost identical to the song Seth has been playing from the bathroom doorway, but through the creature's lips, the tune is smooth and melodious, nasal whine devoured.

I blink and Seth is gone, hallucination swallowed.

The Drinker continues to hum as tiny lumps of memory feed down their second throat. They let go like leeches under pressure, popping from skin with a subtle tug. I watch as the sweltering days on dive bar stages fade to black, as all those nights in my childhood bedroom, black and white lyric-filled composition books in hand, flicker and burn. The senior year talent show. Opening for NOFX. The reunion tour. The night he met his only long-term girlfriend after we played with that impressionistic ska band. The song he wrote for my daughter's third birthday. Gone. One after the next, illuminated rooms growing dark, light switches flicked one after the other.

Then there is a stuttering yank, like a fish on a line, fleeing, then reeled towards the docks. The Drinker's proboscis withdraws from my ear with a suckering pop. There is blood trickling down my neck, thin and languorous. The Drinker reaches into the bedside table, disturbing the still liquid perched on top, coming away with a bandage. They lean over, gently placing the wrappings over my bleeding ear, smoothing the adhesive to bare skin, flattening gauze to staunch the flow, care in each movement. They raise their hand to my cheek, wiping away moisture.

I hadn't realised I was crying.

I hadn't…

But why? Why am I crying?

I can taste the reason, there on my tongue, but I can't identify the flavour, the source. What has been taken? What lost?

The Drinker crumples the paper, stowing it inside the folds of their robe.

'Can I see that?' I gesture towards my hidden writing.

'No. Purpose is done. I'm sorry,' they reply before standing, turning their back to me. They pass by the bathroom doorway. I squint. There should be someone there. Someone had been standing in the entrance moments before. I could swear. I can practically see the silhouette. But there is only blank space. A void feeding back into another void.

'Stop searching,' the Drinker says before they step into the hall. 'This will be better. This will be best.'

Then they are gone, leaving me alone with what remains of my past, a clarity and a redacted view, empty picture frames hanging on endless walls.

After a moment, I pour the blue drink down the bathroom sink, watching as the numbing liquid swills and recedes.

I pull the comforter back, easing beneath the sheets.

The next morning, in the hotel lobby, I walk past the men and women in their plush seats, sunrise licking at the expansive glass windows beyond. They droop and sag, bandaged ears pressed against shoulders. It's not the memories lost laying them low. It's the anaesthetic. They are not weighed down with regret, just intoxication.

I can't say the same for myself as I pass the room key to the concierge.

Something tugs at me, some regret I can't name.

My life feels like I've never known joy, just even keel, no highs, no lows. Constant mediocrity.

I want to remember what I came to forget.

The hotel doors are held open by the doorman. He tips his hat as I walk into the humid morning air.

'Be weightless,' he says as I turn towards where my car is parked in the lot. 'You deserve reprieve.'

But he's wrong. I feel heavier than ever, unseen hands pressing tight over both my ears, forcing in the silence, forcing in the empty space. I could drown in the space, like a vacated room. Suffocate.

In the car, I turn on the CD player and listen to a song I've never heard before. The melody is loud and fast and angry, almost like the vocals come from another world. I let the cd play through three times on my ride home. The songs never grow boring. The songs never slow. The songs never make me feel anything more than emptiness, an emotion that should resonate in my chest, but only leaves a hollow cavity. The nasally voice. The muted strings.

A final note rings out and I cut the engine, home before me, front door left wide, my family waving from the threshold. I smile and wave back, that last note swallowed by whatever I left behind at the hotel.

AISLING NÍ CHOIBHEANAIGH NIC EOIN

THE EATING MONTH

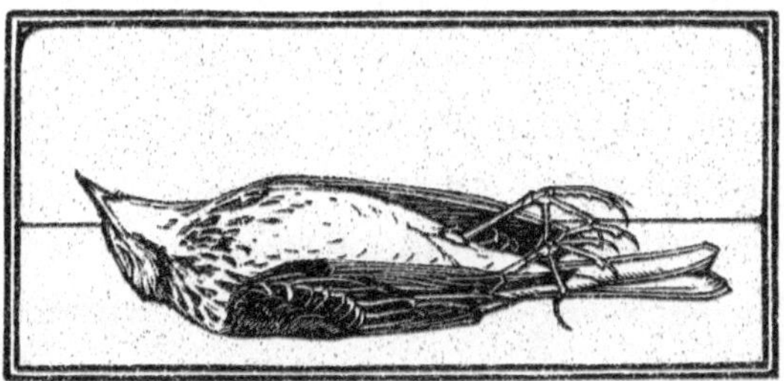

*'Everything that lives and moves about will be food
for you. Just as I gave you the green plants,
I now give you everything.'*
Genesis 9:3

On the morning that he left her, her arms were on top of the duvet, a cold November dawn sharp against her skin. His body thumped against the walls of the house, against the doors; she heard the antique fish vase break, that sharp wail of glass curling in on itself.

Then it was quiet.

The return of that same light, the next October. Her cottage view sinks, muddy with runoff from the Twelve Bens. They stand, shapes that dent the sky, and she stands by the stove looking out as they bring with them sheets of rain. The land rolls out eternally from the window seat in her kitchen, the palette of browns streaked periodically with purple from the heather, or yellow from the gorse. Her only neighbours live on the bend of the road, about a ten minute walk away; an elderly couple. The warmth of lamp light glows from their windows perennially, a glint of yellow against the dark night.

The exterior of her house is sturdy, built to last against the persistent weathering done by Atlantic air. Inside, the walls have been plastered white with a thick brush, the strokes visible even in the gloom of winter light. She is newly unemployed and her days feel short, rising with the sun and examining the changes done to the landscape morning by morning from that window seat. By late afternoon, it is dark again.

It is the eating month for her, the month before a seasonal low mood takes her focus away from food. It is the month where those last good pieces of fruit from the garden must be eaten. Of fatty bacon rinds, of anchovies, slimy against her fingers. Jars of tart beets, those white strings in the flesh of beef. She eats them all, the insatiability of seasonal exhaustion coming at her like a burn on the skin. She prepares for it like this.

As these weeks pass, jars and bags and boxes of things are brought into the house, eaten. Salty like those mistaken breaths that happen underwater, that go deep into your sinuses. Choked down. Greasy smears in her hair, on the neck of her t-shirt. Elbows on the table, hands working through root vegetables and the drippings of meat, little crumblings of hot pastry. It is a full-bodied affair. She pulls at chicken thighs, the translucency of hardened fat shining her teeth into little opals – picks at whatever remains in her mouth with her pointer finger. It is like an embalming; tissue knits itself over this expanding lining of adipose, brining her body for winter.

She watches the sky sink over the jagged wall at the end of the garden.

And somewhere out across these mountains, *he* moves

and sleeps

and eats.

He was an idea to begin with, someone she knew of. She knew of his penchant for recycled furniture and ornithology. Knew of him in the same way that everyone in this area knew of each other. From that, he became flesh. Grew from one knowable shard of bone, coming into her life with a quick mouth.

They were friends. She learned to cook vegetarian meals for him, given that he wouldn't eat meat.

Not even chicken? she asked earnestly when he broke the news.

Not even chicken, he replied, head shaking.

Then they were no longer friends. Tongue on tongue, and an unfamiliar bruising, a softening of her heart. Tenderised, she took him into herself, took in that taste of wool clothing and wet air. Mouth on mouth, seeking that intensity of feeling that was held in his strange words, his strange breaths. She worshipped those words, those breaths, her knees on the wooden floor.

In those months, she looked out at dark patterns in the sky, the murmurations of a species he knew so much about. She learned of beak lengths and migratory patterns, learned to guess what direction this rippling shadow might go in next.

The feeling, he called it, when she guessed correctly. *You've got the feeling.* Sometimes she believed him, imagining that, as she looked out onto a huge and expanding sky, her body could sense some swelling of energy, something akin to the rush of blood that goes to your face in the heat. She would catch it in her throat, a sense that they were approaching a turn or a drop, something that told her to turn or drop herself. Not to risk being left behind. In the end it was just guesswork, and she was wrong as often as she was right, but the wonder she felt in the evenings after those long walks was significant.

She carried the electricity of their observations home with her, skin prickling as she remembered their fluid sinking and rising. Her body gave off gentle twitches as she lay beside him, like the ghost of a motion that was never played out, crushed before it took to the world.

He left her in November.

The room darkens in that strange October way, everything in green. As she looks out at it, the sky flings its last shreds of light upwards, illuminating everything from beneath.

This Sunday's roast is a hot carcass of fat and juice. Her mouth against it, she thinks about this day; *the Lord's day*, as her mother would call it. The Lord's day was Mass in the morning – the backs of her thighs cold against a wooden pew. It was meat and potatoes, the radio singing out the Angelus bell that pulled together even the most distant parts of the parish. It was an inherited faith, or the inherited behaviours of a faith that seemed to be drifting out of daily life.

Where does her faith land on this table of picked-apart food? She is alone, not only in body but in spirit – wading through the emptiness of this old house, her hands deep in the sludge of negative space. She is cyanotype, the clean shape of her body wiped out of its background from the sun's rays, quivering against the blue image of this world. A phantom. She ruminates on this, wiping the grease from her mouth with a sleeve.

Out beyond the patio of the house is a wide nothingness into which her inner self seems to flow, next to all the brightness of the living world. Is this faith then, or some form of it? To kneel in prayer with those sharp juts of light that make up what we see, themselves a community.

The plants begin to wither in the front garden as an early storm brings miserable amounts of rainfall and wind with it. She buries two rooks, crushed under the collapsed woodshed in which they were sheltering, marking their graves with pinkish stones from the shore. On the northerly breeze she senses the approaching winter. And on that breeze strange words return to her, echoes from some far-off time, some place she can no longer access:

> *I am a child in that grove of wind-bent trees. By an*
> *upturned belly of a crab, stranded when the water went out. I*
> *am a child in the cruelty of abandonment, the cruelty of being*
> *left behind. I am those growing yellows and whites on the sea*
> *rock. That same sea rock, brushed smooth by years of tidal*
> *breaths. I am the God light, spheres of yellow softening into*
> *the cloud, into the edges of winter.*
> *I am animal, perhaps. Child, insect, plant*
> *matter, debris. I am sinking in that same left-behind*

seaweed as it dries out, putrid in smell. Flies circle
me, I feel their feet on the strands of me.
I am this crouching form, my spine bent, arms
around my knees. I am the lichen on dead branches,
creatures moving in and out of the hollow parts of me.
I am teeming with all the ugliness of life, and all its
vast beauty.

Her sleep is broken each night by spells of thought that drift between the conscious and the unconscious — time, as the black outline of a man, moves over her bed and onto the ceiling above her. Reaching out to touch him, she feels the warm breath of a recent present on her. One recent present after the next; it occurs to her that life is an eternally generating series of *right nows*. One becomes another, then another, then another. We lift threads from these images of our lives and we weave them out ahead of ourselves to create some vision of what a *then* might look like, but by the time we reach it we are too late. There is nothing behind us or in front of us; we enter each new moment as unprepared for its shape as if we had never thought about it at all.

She watches as the hugeness of organic patterns expand around her, mycelial connections forming between her own body and the bodies of things around her: the open mouth of a dog, the fevered motions of larvae in those flattened rook bellies, the jagged rocks at the side of her house, themselves a home to an uncountable number of things. She wakes in the small hours of the morning, unhungry.

It is a new month.

Outside, a fine rain shimmers under the porch light and the first signs of dawn move across the horizon. Standing at the glass doors, she feels the forces of life twitching within her; blood making its various journeys around her body, the soles of her feet cold against the tile, her mouth dry with a strange thirst.

A sharp sound to her left catches her attention, and she turns to face it. On the window is a smudge of some sort, vaguely illuminated by the light. It almost seems to move when she approaches it, as if her intrusion into its sphere of colour and shape has had an effect.

'Strange weather,' she says, realising that it is the first time she has spoken in some weeks. Her mouth is dry and her voice sounds odd, cracking a little from disuse.

As she opens the back door, the fibres from her woollen jumper are coated in a layer of soft damp. There is a saltiness in the air which has been blown in from the sea and which will most likely remain here until the wind picks up again. It is entirely silent, so *loudly* silent, in fact, that she can feel the sound of her own breaths weighing down the world around her. The porch light casts her image onto the dark glass of the window, and in it, she notices that the mist of water around her head is a painted shade of gold. On the ground below the window, a mass of feathers and mangled wings.

There you are.

He quivers a little, particles of damp air sticking onto the peaks of exposed feathers, to that fluff on his stomach. She bends, taking him into her cupped hands and feeling that warmth which is so much sharper before death. Like some tiny heart, he beats gently against her skin, legs quivering, beak open. His head turns itself inwards, nudges itself under her thumb, and then he is still.

The agitations of a new faith swell in her heart, massive and painful. In this moment, she can apprehend the briefest and most transient communions of spirit; as if little shards of it have been scattered amongst each piece of her current reality and now, reunited with a missing slice, she can see it all. It is uncertain, ready to collapse if even one thing should change.

She presses her face against him. That familiar softness ripe against her nose, her eyelashes, her lips. She can imagine him as before; dressed in wool, long hair wild against the mountain air.

She holds him against her mouth, the last shreds of his heat mingling with hers. Under the porch light the rain resembles threads of fine silk rather than discrete drops. They continue to knit themselves together, creating a web that joins the enormous view of everything around her. It is all one.

Mouth against his body, she speaks to him in the gentlest of voices, the smell of this damp body in her nose, in her throat. *I am this crouching form, my spine bent, arms around my knees.* Then she takes a tender bite of those feathers, through them. He is sweet, like the skins of fruit and yet he tastes of the sea. He tastes of that exposed crab belly, of algae growing outwards in yellows and whites and blues, of seaweed strands and tall plumes of wind-swept grass. Of this great web, knitting itself out beyond what she can see and what she can hear, pulling everything into her. Of the bleeding out of this season — its final moments held here in her fingers.

Those first hours of November are brightening over her body and on him, she can taste the muted stirrings of daybreak.

MALL

RAT

'Talk about depressing,' her brother, Ben, says as he approaches the husk of Ready-Set-Toy. Without a backlight, the store's signage looks more black than the vibrant red of memory. 'Christ, I can almost hear those motoriSed pets they had by the entrances. You know, I always wanted that little ferret with the ball.'

'I had one,' Jess says, snapping his photo for the thumbnail. She lowers her camera. 'It's probably somewhere in Mom and Dad's basement.'

'Maybe it's worth something now.'

'Doubt it.' She checks her watch; it's almost three-fifteen, and the Perry Group wants the keys returned by five. '*Shit*.' She punches the record button. 'Let's move.'

Ben's clutching the straps of his backpack like an overeager schoolboy. 'Fine, but I ain't running,' he says, sidestepping her. 'We've got time.'

But they need plenty of footage. A seamless shift in online content, from low-traffic to abandoned malls, one kind of dead mall to the other, calls for thorough exploration. Too drained from the three-hour drive to reiterate, she follows him in silence to a steel-framed map display.

The directory below the floor plan lists Lake Juniper Plaza's final roster of businesses. Some have folded nationally in the fourteen years since 2011 – victims of the retail apocalypse like Ready-Set-Toy. One store in particular catches her eye. 'There's a Mauve,' she says.

'An actual one?'

Jess taps the store name in response.

'Let's pick you up some black nail polish,' Ben says, slinging his arm around her. 'We'll revive your *emo* era.'

'You can fuck right off,' she replies with a smile. That style (swooped hair, skinny jeans, dark eyeliner) died with the noughties and the Mauve of her teen years. In a rebrand to Vault, the company replaced its iron chandeliers with hanging light bulbs, its alt-rock background music with indie folk.

Ben teases her about the time she repurposed safety pins into earrings. His laughter echoes throughout the murky corridor.

She half-chuckles, cheeks burning, although she has no regrets. After all, the look afforded her teenage self a sense of identity. The realisation of how long it's been, however, stirs a seasick feeling within her as she turns onto the main concourse.

A filthy, latticed atrium caps the walkway. Urn-shaped planters house dead foliage. Gnaw marks zigzag across the ancient white walls. Rats. She shudders at the thought of them scaling the facades and nibbling the plaster.

And yet, the retro charm she finds in the sloped cornices, in the toothpaste-blue tiles spanning the floor, somehow puts her mind at ease. She hasn't seen such an aesthetic since the Aura Mall, the subject of the college film that launched her career. Ten years later, nine since Aura's demolition, she's still exploring malls with her brother, her on-screen talent since day one. *Ten years already.*

'Holy shit,' says Ben.

She shakes off the reverie and halts before a puddle of broken glass, once a store window. Shards crunch under Ben's Air Jordans. 'Looters,' he says, peering inside. 'So much for us being the first ones here.'

'Who the hell loots a Zelocity's?' A business that caters to preteen girls, nowhere near as popular as it was in the '80s, seems like a strange target.

He snorts. 'Someone looking for left-behind lip gloss? Anyway, we'll get decent footage inside.'

Rat-squeamish though she is, Jess knows a half-assed video will hardly garner the views or revenue they need to keep the channel alive. 'You first,' she tells him.

Upon entering, she's struck by a sour, mildewy stench, then by the relics of the former tenant. The walls are still pink; a yellowed poster on a support pillar announces a sale from another time. Jess focuses her camera on its faded font. Her fingers thump as she remembers rummaging through display boxes for candy-coloured nail polishes.

'Jess, come here a minute?'

Her vision ripples before she spots Ben behind the counter, beside a cracked door to a storage room. She pads over to him and says, 'Please tell me you didn't break your way in.'

'It was unlocked.' He shoves open the door and enters with his flashlight.

At the threshold, she watches the narrow beam trace spider webs and water stains. The light swings left, landing on a large cavity, and an exodus of rats flashes through her mind. 'What the hell?' she says, rediscovering her voice. 'Looters did this?'

'Nah, this was scrappers.' He steps closer. 'Probably after the piping.'

'Not copper wires?'

'If that were the case, the store's walls would've been torn up.' The opening swallows the glow. 'Damn, it's like a prison tunnel.' He turns and wags the light at her. 'Well, come on.'

Jess slides the flashlight from her windbreaker's pocket and clicks it on. No rats, but the walls appear more gnawed than those outside. She tiptoes over to Ben and, with a deep breath, looks up from her camera.

The tunnel, spacious enough to crawl through, runs deep into the mall. Its sides are smooth, seemingly eroded – but wouldn't that require an external force? For a moment, she catches a whiff of cinnamon, and her thoughts swim to the Aura Mall, where poor ventilation near Penny's Pretzels would leave the air thick with the scent. Bittersweet butterflies swarm in her belly. Ben yammers on, unbothered, while she juggles past and present, mall pretzels and the pleasant electricity coursing through her. Now her cheeks hurt from smiling.

Ben's at her heels, asking what's wrong, if she saw a rat. She shakes her head and reminds him they don't have all day, then beelines for the open storefront. It's almost four, and Mauve's near the food court, at the other end of the mall.

Down the walkway she runs, passing blemished walls bright with sun. She licks sweat from her lips when she sees Mauve, its studded purple arch reminiscent of Aura's.

'Jess, did you hear that?'

'Hear what? Hold this a second?' She gives him the camera.

'I thought it was rain,' he says, 'but the sky's clear.'

She cups her hands to the window and, staring inside, imagines the walls honeycombed with t-shirt displays, imagines speakers pulsing songs by Paramore, My Chemical Romance, and Fall Out Boy.

'We ought to keep going,' he says, beside her now. The channel, in need of content and views, crosses her mind; then Ben grabs her arm.

The clicking sound, noticeable now, peels her eyes from the glass. Inexplicably drowsy, she looks to her right, where a woman spiders across connected storefronts; a waif in leg warmers.

Matted grey hair hangs from her scrunchied high ponytail. She leaps from the facade, and bits of wall flake from the holes left by her talons. Needle-like, pink with a polish that matches her sweatshirt, her nails tick the tiles as she crawls on all fours towards a planter. She drops something from her jean skirt inside.

Curiosity piqued and too groggy to move, Jess watches her gaze into the muck like a child awaiting magic at a wishing well.

'*Jess!*' Ben hisses.

The woman spins around; her glossy lips pinch at their edges, revealing curved yellow teeth. But her stare floats past them.

Jess pivots, bleary-eyed; the staccato claw-clatter behind her fizzles into white noise. *Ben?* He's no longer on her arm; his screams grow distant. Yet here she remains, entranced by her reflection on the shop window. It sparkles like lake water, drawing her in closer before ageing in reverse. Little by little, the fine lines around her smile smooth; her hair and clothing sift through styles until she sees herself at seventeen, clad in a Paramore shirt and grey jeans, black bangs sweeping across her forehead.

For this Jess, worries amount to pimples and report cards; she can smell cinnamon sugar without thinking about content and revenue.

She stares down at her hands; the skin, too creased for a teen, unmasks the illusion. And then there's her clothes: the windbreaker and sweatpants she pulled from her closet that morning.

The glass has lied; it only hides the crow's feet, the slight slump of her shoulders. She wants to look away. Wants to, but cannot. She leans in closer. There's something off about the girl before her. But what? Then it hits her: she looks incomplete without her eyeliner. Unable to bear this, she careens to the nearby planter and reaches inside. The dry dirt chills her fingertips as she smears it under her lashes.

Retrieving more, she notices a glint.

Embedded in the soil are two safety pins.

She steps over the camera Ben's meant to be holding, then leans into the storefront window and jabs a pin through her left earlobe. She leaves it unclasped the way she used to, with the point angled upward.

A wail – a plea for help – booms from nearby. The second pin lingers in her pinch until her eyes refocus; grinning, she drives the barb through her earlobe.

Her reflection cracks; glass explodes, and from the murk, a guitar slide screams. Mouthing the words, she follows the song over shards, into Mauve. Breath ragged with anticipation, she wanders across the concrete floor. Euphoria rises from her belly, the sensation like a roller-coaster thrill, as though My Chemical Romance is playing to her alone.

She pauses at the back wall, the source of the music, and realises this is where she belongs, where the old Jess wants her. She knows this like the lyrics she's muttering. When she reaches out to feel the vibration, her hand passes into deeper darkness. She hoists herself into the cavity and, inching forward, feels the tunnel contort to her shape. Here, protean music flows. Songs meld and shift in a kaleidoscope of sound. Her excitement burns into a dreamy warmth. The tunnel floor cushions her palms and knees. Her eyelids gain weight, her limbs become numb, and she feels herself drift towards a tangible place where black chandeliers loom.

'No sign of them here, chief, but there's something… looks like a tunnel. Hold on–'

Her eyes flick open to a pitch-black world. Her back aches, and there's no music.

'Teagues?' the same voice says, softer than before. 'You alright?' She hears footsteps. 'Teagues, *hey!*'

Another round of footsteps, then silence.

Desperate for time to bend again, she remains still, waiting, until something brushes her cheek. It's too dark to see, but the object she caresses has a playing card's dimensions. Perplexing as this is, she yields to a protective urge, slips the item in her pocket, and then smells cinnamon. Cinnamon sugar. Like a bloodhound trailing the scent, she crawls backwards through the tunnel, darts across Mauve, and emerges from its storefront. She squints against the floodlight shining down on a taped-off camera. Richer than before, the smell reclaims her attention, and she chases it down through the moonlit mall, sweat streaming down her temples.

Neither cop notices her duck behind the planter.

'Teagues,' says the taller man, jostling the shorter one, who has his hands against the store window. 'The hell's wrong with you?'

When he shakes him again, she recalls the yellow tape around the camera.

Her camera.

And then it dawns on her: they're here for her, to separate her from her past, to close off the passage, her tunnel, and all the veins running through the walls. Lake Juniper knows this; it's been whispering warnings with songs and cinnamon. Yes, she sees how it is.

'Get off!' the shorter man wails, wriggling in his partner's hold. 'Clegg, you bastard, let me go! Let me the *fuck* go!'

If she stands by, she'll be next – yanked away and thrown back to the present.

No. She won't allow that. Can't allow that.

The taller man, seeing her in the reflection, releases his partner and whips around. She shields her eyes from the beam's brightness.

'Wait,' he croaks, approaching. 'Jessica? Jessica Pond?'

So he *is* here for her. He recognises her. But how? She's young again, her old self. Isn't she?

He'll take you away. The internal voice accompanies a harsher pretzel aroma, the spice of which almost burns her nostrils. *He'll take you away.* The realisation sends her shrieking, crashing into him.

His flashlight clatters to the floor, its glow gleaming off her black nail polish as she claws his face. She smells no cinnamon, only coffee-breath screams.

His fist collides with her cheek.

He'll take it all away. 'I won't let him,' she murmurs, then brings his head down against the tile. The impact reverberates before the mall exhales to silence. Moonbeams churn the walkway's gloom. Against the serene stillness, she stands, breath steadying, and wipes her hands on her jeans.

Instinct leads her fingers to her pocket, and she extracts the item the mall has given her. A Pokémon card. The foil behind the creature's wings shimmers with grounded torchlight. Her brother had this one; he always liked the fire types.

The thought fades when a girl wearing leg warmers strikes her mind's eye. Jess turns, fidgeting with the safety pin in her left ear, towards the storefront, where the other man, Teagues, hovers before his reflection — a boy, bespectacled and mousy. A former self, still young.

She looks down at the card again, a fragment of many a '90s childhood, hers included. But the piquant-sweet scent from the closest planter confirms it belongs to him. The boy who's watching her.

Maybe this is how the past becomes the present – through memories and the paths they open. She knows what to do now, reckons this is how reflection and reality combine.

Piano chords and wounded vocals erupt the second she places the card in the planter. The song's nostalgic melody beckons her back to Mauve. Her pulse flutters with the drumbeat as she races for the floodlight. And when a window bursts behind her, she sings louder but presses on; her voice carrying through the dust and shadows of Lake Juniper.

G R U B

CATERPILLAR

Their community inhabits a series of treetops connected by bridges, and so Tonina is eleven when her feet first touch the soil.

'Eleven's a good age to go down to harvest,' her father says. 'Same as your ma.'

Her father has been saving up the good noos-paper, all crinkly and black-and-white lined, and folds it into a hat as they eat breakfast. He only knows two paperfolds: hats and little rowboats. Both look remarkably alike. After he places the hat on her head, he rubs at the creases in her shirt. 'You'll do alright, Nonie. I'll make your favourite for supper.'

She descends the rope ladder. The soil is spongy and uneven under her shoes. She steadies herself, grinning at the way the afternoon light marbles against her fingers.

They stop and set up a few ladders against the largest tree trunk, the one that holds nearly a third of their community off the ground. Every time her hands disappear under a leaf, she bites her lip bloody waiting for a nip from lurking snakes.

The sack slowly fills with perfect yellow globes of mothfruit. She wonders at how it tastes.

Every time her hands tremble, Nonie tells herself to stop being silly – knows that her ma must face worse than string-thin snakes on her travels. She hasn't much memory left of her, but she does remember the things her ma Finds. Last time, it was a bag full of paint and paper, bright coloured thread and candlewax; all as pretty as her ma's bright hair. Pretty, glittering things that her father picks out every morning to sell at the market.

Her father always says it's alright to be scared. It only means that her body is being sensible.

When Nonie descends the ladder with another armful of mothfruit, she finds herself alone on the forest floor.

The pattering of rain means the darkness makes sense. Nonie thinks of her ma again as she draws closer to the tree – of a rusty sword she brought back from the Finding once, that had been too heavy for Nonie to hold. Nonie doesn't know what she would do with the sword if she had it now, but she wishes she did. She stuffs the fruit into her pockets, hooks her arms around a vine, and brings herself up off the ground. She counts under her breath and longs for her father's dumpling soup as she waits for the rain to ease.

A wet leaf sticks against her shoulder, and she shrieks, but no bite comes. When she unscrews her eyes, the leaf is actually a pitcher plant, and nestled within it is a tiny blue grub. Better yet — there's another mothfruit growing there, cuddling into the tree trunk. It's so pristine, it's like a little sun.

All the mothfruit goes to the silkworks, and Nonie knows they'll pay her a whole extra three bits if she comes back holding this one. But the day has put her in a stormy mood. She picks up the grub and puts it atop the yellow globe. It dutifully chomps into the flesh, marring it.

Nonie smiles. A bead of liquid comes up from the puncture; she collects it on her thumb and sticks it in her mouth. It's the sweetest thing she's ever tasted. It's only remembering her father's advice (not to eat things she finds on the ground or in the trees without telling him first) that stops her from cupping the fruit in her hands and devouring it whole. She curls the grub around her finger and encourages it back onto a flat, furry leaf.

Later, Nonie peeks her head out, finds the rain has stopped, and gathers herself up. The grub takes one long moment to mourn, and then drops into the crease of her hat.

In Nonie's rush to sit for dinner, she clatters her things down on the tabletop. The grub, fat with mothfruit leaf, slumbers for a time, but the clink of Nonie's spoon on the empty bowl wakes it up. It bites experimentally into the noos-paper. Although it makes sturdy hat material, it isn't quite as tasty as the hatching leaves. The kitchen scent draws it upwards, in search of more to eat.

Nonie's father is elbow-deep in soap suds. He doesn't notice Nonie's squeak as the grub makes itself known. She admires the markings on his back: silver rings not unlike the ones on her father's hob. The rest of him is a strange dark blue, like the colour the night sky goes when it feels like dressing up.

'What is it, Nones?' her father asks, when their conversation stilts and then stops. 'You're not unwell?'

Nonie is not particularly good at keeping secrets. She holds her hand out, and the grub tickles her as it climbs over her palm. 'I'll take him back down tomorrow,' she says.

'Where did you get him?' her father asks.

'He climbed out of my hat,' she says. 'Maybe he fell in when I was on the harvest.' Her father's face has a strange expression on it, and so she says again, 'I promise, I'll take him back tomorrow.'

Her father reaches out for the grub, and she places it into the square of his palm. 'No,' he says, quietly. 'I think you should keep him. He looks like a very important fellow, don't you think?' He lifts Nonie's hand up for her to take the grub back. 'But keep him a secret for now, alright? Don't tell anyone on the harvest about him. Not just yet.' When she nods, her father goes back to the dishes, humming a tune she doesn't recognise under his breath.

Every day, she smuggles a handful of mothfruit leaves into the front pocket of her overalls, and once her shift has finished, the grub tickles her hand with its head, asking for dinner. But somehow, she doesn't expect him to grow.

COCOON

When the other children abandon Nonie to the forest-dark again and again, she starts smuggling chunks of stolen mothfruit from her palm into the brim of her hat. The fruit looks delicious, and the juice is sweet, but the flesh tastes like the dust under old furniture. Still, the grub devours it before it soaks the noos-paper, and so her crimes are never discovered.

By the time Nonie turns fourteen, Grub has grown to the length of her arm, and is four times as thick. Even though she stops wearing the noos-paper hats, he manages to stow away in her clothing, clinging to the back of her dress when he gets too big to be smuggled in the seams of her overalls.

He does not remain a secret for very long.

At sixteen, when she grows too tall for the mothfruit harvests, Nonie instead becomes a fixture at their family's market stall. Her father's never liked the crowds; Nonie doesn't either, but would never tell her father that. But Grub – oh, Grub *loves* the market. If worms could preen, she imagines he would. The silver rings on his back grow even shinier, and he curls up atop the table to watch the yellow-garbed crowds pass by their dwindling pile of wares.

The people don't want heaps of metal. They want the yellow silk from the silkworks. It's cloth Nonie has seen all her life and only recently has realised she will never afford. Grub insists on being carried, which leaves slimy marks on her clothes that don't quite come out with soap. The people look at her oddly; her market table remains full. She makes enough coin to pay for the flour for their dumplings and for the bruised and rejected mothfruit they feed Grub for dinner, but never enough for silk.

By now, Nonie has nearly grown into her height, into her sticky-out ears – and even, sometimes, into the name Tonina. One afternoon, a group of youths come by and ask if she wants to join them down in the depths of the tree. Most of them give up quickly, except for a person she's never noticed before: lingering, smiling at her until the corners of their eyes crinkle up. They even offer to pay for her drinks. Nonie looks down at Grub: too heavy to carry in her arms, and too slow to follow at her heels in a throng of people. She shakes her head. The youth's yellow cloak ripples as they depart. Once they're gone, she sinks back into her chair.

Soon, she goes home. 'Da,' she says.

'Good day?' he says, pressing a kiss to her forehead.

'No,' she says and crumples up.

'Just wait.' He cups her head in his hands, his palms rough as tree-trunks against her cheeks. 'Just wait for your ma. She'll bring riches you can't imagine. It'll change our fate.' His smile is earnest, and it hurts. 'You'll see.'

Bright sun intermingles with rain on the day that the riders come back from the Finding. Nonie sits under the awning of the market stall and tries to smile for the passing customers, tracing the hob-rings of Grub's back. A shadow passes overhead. Then comes another. She hauls Grub up into her arms, then skids over to the lookout point. The light licks at her bare shoulders, makes her squint – but the giant moth wings make up for it, paling the rainbows behind them into insignificance.

She abandons the table entirely. The riders flock down, down, to land. There's at least twenty of them, all grown — around her father's age. They start passing out pretty things to their kin: metal cylinders with drawings of tart green fruit on them, blankets with feather-light stitches, a curious glass orb which looks like a bubble made permanent. Nonie immediately covets a fragile, orchid-like insect that will later sell at market for three times the price of an orchid, and have a lifespan a third as long.

Amongst all the colours in the world being passed between the riders' fingers, her ma's red hair is nowhere to be seen.

Nonie stands there at the landing for hours, watching the skies until they turn from blue to pink to black, and then when only the stars come out to fill the murk. The muffled sounds of celebration float up between the thick branches of the tree, but Nonie can do nothing but sob into the soft linen of her sleeve.

The next morning, when the youth in the yellow cloak wanders over and asks if Grub is for sale, she asks them to name their price.

It only takes a handful of minutes for Nonie to regret her words. Over the course of the morning, Grub stops chirruping. In the afternoon, she notices that his slime has stopped catching the light. By evening, her suspicions are confirmed; Grub's silvery hob-rings have somehow dulled in the sunlight, and he screws himself up into a ball every time she tries to pick him up.

She goes to her father, who is counting out forks in a corner of the house and sighing. For a moment, she hesitates, but it spills out. 'I think Grub is sick.'

'I thought you did not like him,' he says. 'But you cry, Nonie.'

'I don't,' she sniffs. 'I don't like him, a lot of the time. I don't like that I can't have a life like the others. But he is mine, and this *is* my life, and so I must look after him.'

In the smattering of days that follow, Nonie opens the stall only twice. Grub now must be hefted there in one of her mother's rejected rucksacks. Her father, repairing their fence, murmurs that they will survive the loss of income that week. The third day that Nonie tries to go to the market, Grub cannot even follow her out the door. She tucks him into bed next to the fire and bribes a child into bringing some mothfruit leaves back from the harvest.

When she awakens the next morning, Grub has gone.

Nonie finds her father outside, binding a horrible grey lumpen mass to the new fence with ribbons. 'I brought him out here at dawn,' he says, gesturing for her to help him tie the knots. 'He'll need space to spread his wings, you see.'

MOTH

They sit with the cocoon until Nonie's father has run out of words.

'It used to be that children weren't sent down for the moth-fruit, but for caterpillars. And it used to be that all the children in the village found a caterpillar, if the season was right and the mothfruit crop grew well enough to sustain them. Your ma found hers on her second trip down, and she was the pride of her family for months. Imagine my pride when you found yours on your first!'

'But no one else has a Grub,' says Nonie.

'The yellow cloth makes more coin. The fruit started being taken to the silkworks for dyeing, and so there haven't been new caterpillars in the undergrowth for years.'

At this, an odd, melancholy weight settles along Nonie's spine. She leans her head against her father's shoulder. For the first time, she notices grey coming through in the dark of his beard. 'I'm not quite sure what will happen, Nonie,' he says. 'But we'll learn together.'

He tells her what little he knows: that Grub is dissolving into mush that might become moth, and that the stories she shares with him as he remakes himself anew are important. Nonie trades a pair of silver earrings for books and takes to sitting by the cocoon and talking to it. She wonders if somewhere in that pile of goo, Grub might be able to hear her. When she is not sitting by the cocoon, she's waiting at the lookout point for a streak of red hair on the horizon. Her ma has done this before, would tell her *how* to do this. But her ma is not there.

Her father is. Her father, who taught her to write, daubing colours on the walls of the kitchen with her fingers, who made her old noos-paper hats out of strange black-and-white squiggly paper. Now, he is there rigging up bigger and better supports as the cocoon hardens, so that she might spend more time telling Grub stories of all the places he might go to once he has wings. Even as she tells these tales, she never imagines that he will want her to go too.

She turns seventeen and then eighteen. Nonie becomes Tonina properly on the day she trades away the last of their forks. She ignores the yellow cloth the merchant offers her, and instead exchanges them for sheets of noos-paper. She spends her evening murmuring through the columns and hopes that Grub will not know that she makes half of it up, where the words have rubbed away.

And still, the cocoon remains unchanged. And Tonina's ma does not come home to help her.

Tonina is woken early one morning near her nineteenth birthday by her father shaking her awake. Outside, the first fingers of dawn have begun pinking the sky. It's enough light for her to see that the cocoon has begun rippling.

'What do we do?' she says, clutching at her father's elbow.

'We wait,' he says, and there's a quiet smile in his sloe-dark eyes.

They settle in. The people rise for their breakfast and find Tonina and her father curled up on the walkway outside their house, and know what is to come. It is mid-morning before the cocoon breaks, and a new creature crawls out, leaving behind such a dry dead thing that Tonina wonders how she ever gave it her heart. This new creature is huge; its body tufted with night-sky fluff, still sticky-matted from the cocoon.

When she turns, her father is binding a long stick to the fence with a length of torn cloth. Tonina runs and trades her entire pile of books for an eighth of a mothfruit, and uses it to encourage this new creature to climb up the stick. The wind is playful, ruffling the fluff on the creature's body.

As the wings begin to unfurl, the crowds grow, until their little walkway is more crowded with people than she's ever seen. Tonina stands in front of the perch herself for hours, arms folded, even as the arches of her feet ache and send tremors up her calves. Her father wheels round a cart with a pot of steaming dumpling soup, selling bowlfuls of it to the spectators.

'You encourage them,' says Tonina, but her anger is only surface-deep. The purse at his hip clinks happily with bits.

'They too need to be fed, Nonie. They'll move on,' he says. 'Eventually.'

'Doesn't he need peace and quiet to dry his wings out?'

'He spent half his childhood peering over that market stall, enjoying the crowds. I'm sure he's enjoying giving a show.'

The wind picks up. The crowds retreat inside. She and her father stand there, alone, eating the last of the soup. As the sky becomes the same dusky-blue of the creature's wings, it turns its head to look at her.

For a moment, Tonina is Nonie again, sharing that small part of herself, looking to see if there's any recognisable part of this new creature. She wonders if he recognises her. And then she sees that his wings have unfolded to reveal the pattern of shining silver rings, and that it *is* Grub after all, watching her.

He flaps his wings, crawls a few tentative steps up the pole, and then flutters down onto the walkway in front of them. The breeze picks up the fronds in his antennae. His head tilts towards her.

'Climb up,' says her father, smiling wetly at her. 'Go on. You'll do fantastic, Nonie. And when you come back, I'll make your favourite for supper.'

She goes. Flight becomes both her greatest joy and her worst guilt. She will go again the next day, high enough this time to look upon the tree-top canopy that has been her home for her whole life, only to realise that the towering branches now seem twig-sized. The people are yellow mites, swarming.

The day after that, she will pack her meagre things into one of the many rucksacks left behind in their house. But it will only be a short trip. Grub is not yet big enough to carry another passenger. She'll return with her bag full of brown-paper parcels: herbs, salt, vegetables. As her da rolls up the dough in their now-uncluttered kitchen, Tonina will begin to take his old dumpling cart to pieces, cobbling together something that could one day be strapped to Grub's fluffy body. She'll paint a sign and buy undinted pots and pans from the Finding.

And then one day, much later, they'll go.

DO NOT STARE AT THE SUN

I wake up on the floor next to the bed.

'Morning, Len.'

The voice is chipper and comes from somewhere outside my head, above me. I ignore it and hold my eyes shut. The darkness is warm and comforting. It is viscous, moving, rotating slow and heavy.

I open my eyes and my vision spins. Shooting pains inside my brain, along my arms, down my legs.

I taste bleach, and something else, metallic. I can't place it. I feel heavy too, weighed down.

'Morning, Len,' the voice repeats. 'Rise and shine.'

I continue to ignore the voice and shift myself up, back against the bed. The room is small, but self-contained: bed, kitchen units, stove, dining table, bookshelves, shower, toilet.

To my left, a door that's been boarded up; on my right, a window that's had the same treatment. In the corner, above the bookshelves, a small speaker.

Head pounding, I say, 'Where am I?'

My arms and legs ache. Unreachable places on my back twist sharply. I pull up the sleeves on my jumpsuit but find no evidence of damage. No bruises, no cuts, just dry skin and a seven-pointed star tattooed on my wrist and a configuration of letters around it: A A A E NA O SA.

'What is this?' I say, and this time I glance towards the speaker in the ceiling.

'Don't worry yourself about that,' the voice says.

'I feel like I should. I don't remember anything.'

'Does your head hurt?'

'Everything does. Why?'

'The best advice I can give is: try not to think about it.'

'Saying that is going to make me think about it.'

'I understand, but try to follow my advice. It's good advice.'

'Okay, then, well, what now? Do I just wait until my memory comes back?'

'I wouldn't worry about that.'

'Why?'

'I cannot talk to you about that.'

'What can you tell me then?'

'Well. You're Len, Len, and it's time for another day.'

'Another day of what?'

The chipper tone is pissing me off, and I suspect it's supposed to.

I remember nothing. I don't know who I am, where I am, or how I got here. I am a blank notebook waiting to be filled.

'If you won't tell me who I am, can you tell me who you are?'

'My name is Buddy,' the voice says, 'and I'm your companion.'

Exhausted, hungry, I sit down on the bed. There's a lamp on the bedside table. I pull open the top drawer and lift out the only item inside: a worn-looking Gideon's Bible.

I open it and it flips open to a less-than-random page, Colossians 2.2: *My goal is that they may be encouraged in heart and united in love, so that they may have the full riches of complete understanding, in order that they may know the mystery of God, namely, Christ.*

I laugh. 'The full riches of complete understanding. How apt.'

'The Bible is a good book, yes,' the voice says. 'The Good Book. It can keep you grounded in times of difficulty.'

'Like when I have no memory of who I am?'

'Exactly.'

I tip the book back to the start. There I find my first clue: a short note written in scruffy cursive that says *Do not stare at the Sun*. I look over at the boarded window, through which no natural light enters, and chuckle. Placing the Bible back in the drawer, I stand up.

'Why can't I remember anything?'

'Try not to worry about it,' Buddy says.

'That's not an answer.'

'It is *an* answer, Len.'

'You know more than you are letting on.'

'All you need to know is that you're Len Ligardi, Len.'

'But *who* am I?'

'Well, that's a different question. And not for me to decide, is it?'

I look at the speaker.

'I found a note on the first page of the Bible. It said "Do not stare at the Sun."'

'Good advice,' Buddy says.

'Did I write that note?'

Buddy ignores me, which I take to mean *yes*.

'You must know more about me.'

I tap the window boards. I give the bottom plank a tug but it doesn't give.

'A solid bit of carpentry there, Len,' the voice says. 'Well done.'

'I did this?'

'Yes.'

'To keep me inside this room?'

'Yes.'

'Why would I do that?'

'For your own good,' Buddy says. 'Sometimes you do listen to me.'

'Is it dangerous outside?'

'Danger is all relative, Len.'

'Well, what kind of dangers are you talking about?'

On the underside of the plank, I find the same message written in the same handwriting: *Do not stare at the Sun.*

'Well, the Sun for one.'

'The Sun.'

'Yes. Because you're on a spaceship, Len, millions of miles from home.'

I close my eyes again and the darkness swells and swoops inside my head.

'Is that why everything feels a little… heavier, I think?' There's a pause. 'Oh, yes, of course. I had to increase the ship's rotation speed by 5% to accommodate the CME that will hit the ship in 11 hours.'

'CME?'

'Coronal Mass Ejection, an expulsion of magnetic energy from the Sun. It can cause damage to the ship, and short circuit electronic devices. It'll be corrected by tomorrow.'

I move across to the door.

'Is there anyone else on board this ship?'

'There is not.'

I try pulling one of the boards, and then bang on it a couple of times. I become breathless almost instantly, and have to stop as my vision blurs around the edges.

I walk over to the stove, tap a few of the surfaces, look in the cupboards.

'Why are all the cupboards empty?'

'I will fill them up for you when you are next asleep.'

'Is there anything I can have now? My stomach is killing me.'

'I prefer to do maintenance when you're asleep. If you get back into bed, and put the duvet over your head, I can bring something in.'

'You won't let me leave to get it myself?'

'I never said you couldn't leave, Len.'

'There are boards on the door, and the window.'

'Like I said, you did that.'

'But why would I do that?'

'For your own good.'

'And if I ask to leave, you won't stop me?'

'No, but I advise against it in the strongest terms.'

I stop for a second. Beneath our conversation I hear a noise. Ticking.

'Where is that clock, Buddy?'

'In Bay 2.'

'So where am I then?'

'Well, you're in Bay 1, but this room is The Bedsit.'

'Buddy, I want to leave,' I say.

'Are you sure about that, Len?'

'I have never been more sure of anything.'

'Okay, Len,' the voice says. 'But it's your choice.'

Somewhere, motors turn and scrape. They shift around in the walls, cawing and hooting. The whole place shudders and, after about fifteen seconds, there's a click and then the four walls pop from their frames, revealing a much larger room.

Bay 1 is double the size of The Bedsit, and mostly empty. It's neat, unsophisticated, and clean. Against one wall there is a door, against another a narrow grey curtain, and somewhere between the two a number of thick weighty-looking barrels. Written on the side of these in a jaunty font is: *Radi-ations: The Food That Will OutLive You*™.

The word *food* slips out of my mouth like a prayer, and I rush over, pulling the lid off the nearest barrel and grabbing the first vacuum-packed pouch from the top of the pile. I twist off the cap and suck out its insides, losing myself to the explosion of taste and feeling.

When the packet is empty, I slide onto the floor and rest against a barrel.

'Wow, you were hungry,' says Buddy.

'When was the last time I ate?'

'Around fifteen hours ago.'

'Was I unconscious that long?'

'I cannot talk to you about that.'

I move over to the curtain and tug at the cable next to it. It rises to reveal a porthole. The porthole has been welded over with a thick plate of metal. I tap it and the echo fills the room. I find the same message on this too: *Do not stare at the Sun.*

'Why do I keep writing this around the ship, Buddy?'

'I cannot tell you that while you are in this part of the ship, Len.'

That's a different answer to before.

I tap the porthole again.

'Have I asked to hear the truth before?'

'You have, Len, and I can assure you it was a mistake then, and it will be a mistake now...'

'No. I want to leave. Let me into Bay 2.'

'Are you sure?'

'I am.'

'As you wish. The door is now open...'

It slides open.

Bay 2 is a near-identical room, but emptier. There are two clocks on the opposite wall, to the left of another door. The first clock is analogue, the source of the ticking, but it has 24 increments instead of 12. It tells me that it is 10am, which by itself means nothing. The second clock is digital and it takes about thirty seconds of staring at it before I realise it's counting down:

112 DAYS, 14 HOURS, 13 MINUTES, 12 SECONDS

...11 SECONDS.

...10 SECONDS.

'What is that counting down to?'

'To your journey's end,' says Buddy from a speaker in the corner.

'That's pretty fucking ominous, is it not?'

He doesn't answer and I cross the room. The digital clock is built into the wall. It has no controls, no buttons. I stare at it for a few seconds and my vision starts to twist. My head shivers with pain, my body shakes, and I slump down on the floor.

'Is there something wrong with my eyes, Buddy?'

'Yes.'

'Can you tell me what happened?'

'I had to operate on them.'

'Why?'

'I can't tell you that, Len. It might give you ideas.'

The clock whispers to me, an anchor to this moment, this place. Except I can hear it better now. It says:

FA

SHIST

FA

SHIST

FA

SHIST

FA

SHIST

'Buddy?'

'Yes, Len.'

'Is the clock calling me a fascist?'

'It might be, Len, but I can't say for sure.'

'I leave a lot of messages for myself, Buddy. How often have you fixed my eyes?'

'I cannot talk to you about that but if you keep asking I will be required to tell you.'

'I want to leave this room, Buddy.'

The door to Bay 3 opens.

There are three tables in the centre of the room, each stacked with papers and photos and small objects. I pick up the first thing I see. A small wooden duck. It's grubby, battered. I recall nothing. I flick through the photos: three friends in a bar, raising a beer, grinning, stood in front of a seven pointed star; in another a toddler, in the arms of a bearded man next to a dark-haired woman; the third is a teenager in a dank room sitting on a couch, beer in one hand, and cigarette in the other; a fourth, a little older, shows a man in a military uniform. The military man's face is identifiable in all of the other photos.

'Is this me, Buddy? Am I a soldier?'

Buddy doesn't answer.

'You're supposed to tell me, Buddy.'

'I know, Len, but all I can do is give answers that I am programmed to say.'

I put the photos down and grab at a worn-out looking document. My birth certificate. Name: Leonard Farnsworth Ligardi. Born 24th February 2304. Father: Harmon. Mother: Davina.

'It's me, right?'

'This is you, Len Ligardi. This is your life.'

'Tell me about myself.'

'I cannot talk to you about that.'

I grabbed at everything on the table: paperwork, photographs, items of clothing, books, jewellery. Still no answers.

'It all fits together to make a story, Len. You just have to know how to tell it.'

I pick up a few letters and read them. Letters from my mother, from old friends, addresses redacted, large chunks of detail redacted, the paper spotted and brown.

I take the photos and spread them out on the floor. I arrange the other items around them and try to take it all in. To create order is to create sense, but to make order you need a basis of understanding.

'If you can't make sense of any of this, nothing I say is going to make this any better.'

'You know who I am.'

'I know you, Len,' which doesn't sound like the direct answer it's intended as. 'Trust me. This is as good as it gets.'

'Let me move into Bay 4.'

I hear a familiar click and when I walk towards it the door opens.

Bay 4 is empty except for a single doorstopper of a book resting on the floor in the middle of the room. I pick it up.

Inside the first page: *Do not stare at the Sun.*

There is no text on the cover or spine, but moving through the initial pages, it appears to be a wealthy man's travelogue through 18th century Italy. I skim through it until I reach the second chapter, where I discover the remaining pages of the book have been replaced with a small monitor.

I tap the screen and it goes on.

'This will give you the answers you want, Len. But not the answers you need. Put it down and let's go back to The Bedsit and play Canasta. I'll actually try and win this time.'

A video starts playing. Warm black fades to a light blue, a flag: the seven pointed star, white and shiny, resting on the foreground of a thick bloody maroon. It fades and then there's a picture of the bearded man and the thin woman. They're holding a baby, me, before fading into the picture from next door. A voiceover speaks:

'Hello Len, and welcome to your life.' The voice is Buddy, but it comes from a small speaker embedded in the screen.

'Leonard Farnsworth Ligardi, born 24th February 2304, on San Francisco, Earth. Harmon was a pharmacist and Davina was a secretary under Dr Landi Boffs at Papel University. From the moment you were born, Harmon was convinced, wrongly, that you weren't his son. Despite your mother's honesty and love, he couldn't shake the feeling. Despite finding no proof of infidelity, he believed it until his dying day, 23rd April 2309, when he was fired from a research post at the Garamond Tech Institute.'

'On that day, he picked you up from nursery then hanged himself in the garage. Your mother found the body, and even though you never saw it, your nightmares were haunted by his corpse. By 14, you were drinking; by 16 you were on drugs. At 17, your mother, unable to handle your addictions, signed you up to the Titan Space Programme in the hope that a regimented lifestyle would straighten you out.'

The screen fades to a map. Over the continent are letters. A A A E NA O SA: Africa, Asia, Arctic, Europe, North Africa, Oceania and South America. The map fades into a seven pointed star and the letters shift to their corresponding points on the star. I pull up your sleeve and my arm, my tattoo, is warm. The video continues:

'You enjoyed the hard work, the camaraderie, and the distance from Earth. You progressed into the Outer Edges Mining Core, joining one of the first teams to explore the Kuiper Belt. It was in these dark reaches that your recovery began to erode. In all that blackness, your mind turned to the light of Earth. To the people you left behind, your home, your dad, the pain. You began to drink again, began to seek out stronger highs. You became hooked on Titan Dust and Zero-G cocaine. Diligence became carelessness and, after 8 years of service, you were dishonourably discharged. From there, you jumped from station to station, taking work wherever it was available, and getting high at every opportunity.

'Things changed in orbit around Mars, on Cantina-B. A chance encounter with UHC's very own John Rimmer led to a life-changing opportunity.'

The screen showed a logo: a tuning fork wrapped in barbed wire, with the words Universal Health Care written in an arc above it.

'John Rimmer told you about his work on Radio-Therapeutics and how he was on the forefront of New Age Solar Medicine. He said he needed volunteers for a new project and told you about a radical new treatment known as Extreme Sun Exposure and you jumped at the chance to be rid of your addictions.'

The screen cuts to various graphs and images of the Sun.

'109 days ago, you boarded a Class-B Escape Pod kitted out with food and an AI Companion. The ship is taking you to within a million miles of the Sun where, through a controlled exposure to its harshest rays, the water in your body and the neo-chemicals that create and maintain addictions will be destroyed.'

'What the fuck?' I say to myself rather than Buddy. 'Did I agree to this?'

'Addiction is complicated, and over the course of 200 plus days, you will feel many things. Anguish, withdrawal, doubt. But you will be safe here with your AI Companion, Buddy. He will look after you. He will ensure that the Memory Suppressant Chip implanted on your skull continues to function.'

'This cannot be right. This cannot be true.'

'The MSC is an important part of the process,' Buddy continues, 'for the neo-chemicals that prevent true recovery will not be able to attach themselves to key memories that trigger your dependencies. When the addiction is gone, your mind will be freed of all the psychotoxins and plurabells that held you back. And we will then, safely, be able to return your memories. All hail John Rimmer. All hail his glorious work, and thank you, traveller…'

The video ends. I stare at the screen for a few seconds.

'So I've done this to myself?'

'I'm sorry, Len.'

'You didn't do this. You're just here to help.'

'I know, but I am supposed to look after you. I keep letting this happen.'

'Wait, how many times have I come to this room?'

'It's been 109 days since we left, and you've reached here about 85 times.'

'Surely this isn't going to work? Surely I'm going to burn to death? Why would I do this to myself?'

'You were desperate, Len.'

'I don't know if it helps, but you told John before you left that you regretted the way you left things with your mother. She was so sad when you told her you were asked to leave the Space Programme. She despaired and that look on her face broke your heart. You told John you'd do anything to make it up to her...'

I sit in silence, turning over these thoughts. Other than the photographs, I cannot picture my mother. I cannot remember her voice, or anything she ever told me.

I stand up and start pacing. I grab at my hair, I begin to shake. Sweat pours from my armpits and my legs and my back. From the other room, I can hear the clock ticking.

KILL

YOUR

KILL

YOUR

KILL

YOUR

SELF

'What am I gonna do? What am I gonna do? What am I going to do?'

'It'll be okay, Len. You just have to believe.'

'What about the notes?'

'The notes?'

'The ones I've been leaving myself. Don't stare at the Sun. What does that mean? Does the Sun do something to me?'

'You don't want to know.'

'I do, Buddy. I want you to tell me.'

'If you insist.'

'I do.'

'It can, if you're in the wrong part of the ship, sometimes, if you're not careful, because of the electro-magnetic radiation, short-circuit the MSC.'

'It allows me to remember?'

'I didn't say that. I am a computer programme. I can't know what it actually does or how it feels for you. All I know is that my systems are set up to respond, to fix it as soon as I can.'

'So if I can break it, I will remember.'

'Yes, I suppose so. But don't you think the fact that you keep leaving yourself these notes suggests that you shouldn't?'

'Are you going to help me with this at all?'

'I've already said too much, Len.'

'You've barely told me anything,' I throw the book and the spine thuds against the floor. It spins, pages splaying like wings, and lands face down. The screen inside hits the ground and, after a second of silence, there's an electrical pop, then static, then Buddy's voice glitching:

'FASH FASH Thi– FASH FASH FASH Thi– Thi– ...This is the story of you. Yes, you, Le– Le– Len Ligardi. Story of. FASH FASH FASH Story of. FASH FASH You. You. You. Bo bo bo born of Har– Har– Harmon, and Dav Davina. –avina –avina –avina.

I pick up the book and the screen is cracked. The seven-pointed star is split down the middle. I hit its side and the video skips.

'...tried and convicted... Geneva Space Convention for Interstellar Crime... sentenced to death by War Crime... Space War... Space Crimes... caused the deaths of over half a million people.'

Images of dead bodies pop up. Photographs of me with a gun, pointing it at the heads of several people. '....the head of the Space Liberation Front... Earthly terror... only way to destroy you was to have you shot into the Sun Sun Sun Sun Sun Sun Sun–'

I slap it again and the footage jumps.

'...refuse to let you become a martyr... -tyr Len Ligar-gar– di' slap slap, 'memory suppressant chip to prevent you from escaping.... Placed in a Class-B Escape Pod... protecting the System from your heinous and rotten ways...'

I look up at Buddy.

'What the fuck is this, Buddy?'

He doesn't speak.

'Seriously, Buddy. What is this? It's saying I'm a fascist? A war criminal?'

'The book is right, Len.'

'But it's now told me two stories!'

'I don't understand what you mean.'

'It said I was an alcoholic being treated by John Rimmer.'

'Indeed you are.'

'But then it told me that I was a leader of a fascist rebellion?'

'I'm afraid that's you, Len.'

'But they both can't be true, surely?'

'I don't know how to answer that, Len.'

'Start talking now before I break every last circuit on board this ship!'

A sound not-unlike a sigh comes out of the speaker.

'Do you know how long you've been here, Len?'

'109 days.'

'Oh, yes, I told you that part. Well, do you know how often you remove yourself from The Bedsit and come through here?'

'Pretty much every day?'

'Correct.'

There's a pause. 'Well?'

'Well, you tell me what that would do to you, Len? It's difficult to deal with you starting from scratch each day. You always realise that this is a horrific and brutal situation. That you're stuck and there's no way of knowing whether you're going to live or die. And on top of that, amongst all the angst and fury that you bring, I've been bored out of my mind.'

'You're bored?'

'I'm an AI, Len. They gave me enough intelligence to protect you from yourself, to do complex surgery when you get injured, and to entertain you as I best see fit.'

'Entertain me? In what way?'

'Both of the stories are lies, Len.'

'You just said they were both true?'

'That was obviously a lie.'

'Why on Earth would you make either of those up?'

'Well, I don't know how to explain this. I don't actually know if they're lies. One of the stories on the tape isn't a lie.'

'How many are there?'

'Hmm, last time I counted, there were about 80 of them. I usually create a new one when this happens. I don't remember which one is the original.

'So I could be an alcoholic?'

'Indeed.'

'Or a fascist?'

'Quite possibly, yes. Or a bio-engineered superhuman who is going to be the first person to land on the surface of a star. Or someone with a degenerative brain condition who is being assisted-suicided-into-the-Sun. Or the guilt-ridden dad of the boy in all those pictures who wants to forget the guilt and the trauma he's given his only child. Or an expert on Coronal Mass Ejections who is going to study one up close, real close, to find the best way to prevent them from destroying all of Earth's technology again. Or a fugitive on the run from Space Cops. Or a—'

'Okay I get it. And there's no way for you to find out?'

'No. Sorry, Len.'

'Well, can you play me the other stories? All the different versions of me you've created?'

'I don't think I should do that, Len.'

'What difference will it make?'

'It won't make you happy.'

'I don't want to be happy. I want the truth.'

'But you won't know the truth either.'

'No, but the truth will be in there, won't it? Even if I don't know for sure.'

'If that's what you want, Len, then pick up the book and I'll feed the stories in one by one.'

I sit down on the floor and open the book. The screen fills with bright darkness at first, and then the seven pointed star and the maroon background and Buddy, videotape Buddy, begins to talk.

He tells me my story over and over. In some of them I am a hero, but in most I am a sad sack, a jerk, an asshole, a delinquent, a tragedy, a farce, a fuck-up. In many of them I am dying, in others I am overworked. In one, I am a harassed middle manager, and in another I am subjugated and restless. He makes me a fascist in several and a communist revolution-ary in others. A peerless genius in one, and a work-shy thief in a few more. In each, I recognise something familiar. There is an overlap, patterns to the ideas that suggest Buddy knows something about my past that can only be drawn out in these fictionalised versions.

'That's the last one,' Buddy says many hours later.

'Thank you, Buddy.'

'Shall we go back to The Bedsit now? The CME is going to hit in about fifteen minutes. You need to be in Bay 1 or 2 so that you are safe.'

I consider this for a second, and then I look towards the door I haven't been through.

'I want to go in there.'

'There's nothing in there, Len. It's an empty room with a window that looks out into space.'

'I want to go in there,' I repeat. 'I need to know for sure.'

'I will open the door for you, Len.'

The door clicks and I walk through. Buddy is right: the room is half the size of the others, and there's an entire wall made of glass. At some point in the last 109 days I have written DO NOT STARE AT THE SUN across it, but I ignore the guy who did that. He doesn't understand what this is like.

I walk up to it and notice there's a small sill. Resting on it is a small black pen. I smile as I slide it into my pocket and look out at the universe. It is dark at first, and the void rotates slow and heavy. Stars reveal themselves and it is magnificent.

Buddy's voice comes through a speaker, saying, 'Five minutes until the Coronal Mass Ejection.'

I ignore it as I must have ignored it numerous times before.

I marvel at the size of the universe. The sheer everything of it all.

'Two minutes, Len.'

I see the twinkles of the Sun against the external beams of the ship. They refract and bounce off my face.

'One minute, Len.'

The ship turns towards the Sun and when the light hits me, it is astounding. Cleansing and beautiful, I open my eyes and let it hit my retinas. There is no protection here and it burns the inside of my skull. I close my eyes again, trap the light inside me, let it spread through my skull like a supernova, digging into every corner. It is the creator, the beginning and end, the alpha and the omega. The god that we are all seeking. It birthed us and it kills us and one day, when it is ready to die, it will consume Earth and we will be returned to it.

'Five seconds, Len.'

I cannot hold my eyes shut any longer. I have to understand. I have to know the Sun, because to know the Sun is to know the Universe. You have to genuflect before it. You have to let it dominate you. It will save me but I have to let it. Encouraged in heart and united in love, I have to have the full riches of complete understanding.

I stand there for an eternity and there is nothing but light. It is everywhere and I am everywhere. Across my vision I see a waveform, a shudder, and then a pop. A dark wave crashes over me and then, suddenly, there is more light and more light and more light, and then, as if waking from a terrible dream, I remember everything.

THE UNDRY

Every damnable day I come here. Have a sup, then another. The time, it goes up in smoke. A grey or yellow haze, depending on the light. Then night's emptiness, the same dreams of the forest. And on and on and on it fucking goes. Thank God for them, these trees. It's the only place around a man can catch a breath. Ahh, taking it in is a treat. Clean air. Well, cleanish. As clean as you're going to get. The smog over by the way is a demon. A gaseous hellbeast of our own making. It's a miracle the lot of us aren't keeled over with them fumes. Maybe you get immune. I never did – I'm a country boy still. It's getting worse for me, if anything. Thought I'd choke on the way here. Got the whiff of bus arse at the crossing. Very nearly landed me on my own arse. Granted, I was shaky enough to start. You'd think they'd decommission those fucking things.

Still, God bless the trees. And the swan that's around too. Most afternoons until late. Any scraps I give to her. To me she brings a calming. Memories I presumed long corroded away. What a gift she is. From another age. Gliding majestic as if she's on a newly-formed, misty lough. Before there were fields. Before canals. Before us and our steaming havoc.

The usual gangs are by the water. Every summer the same. Cans by the canal. Pulled together by nothing but that sweet gravity of youth. Girls with skin so white, and hair so black, you'd swear a wicked witch was going to slip them an apple. Magic. The paper was saying the other day how there's a new type of human every seven years, or some shite. Because of technology, they say. Fuck that. Fuck technology. We're all monkeys rolling in the same sludge. Until they put chips in our brains, or we stop fucking, or we're fucking with metal mickeys, that's what we'll be.

We have the same wants, the same thirst. Night empties day, day fills night, and on it goes.

Daddy had the thirst. Had it fierce in the end. When Mammy died, he took a tumble – we both did. It was on the couch I'd find him most mornings. To make it to bed had become too arduous a trek. That poor couch took the brunt of the old fellow's misery. After jittering the night away on it, he'd invariably end up in some variety of vexed coil-contortion. The most common arrangement was with the neck twisted at an angle, the back turned and humped. On his side, his face would be buried deep – nose-first – within the stench of the corner. It was as though he wanted to merge with the upholstery, to burrow through the fabric, to be encouched. His failure to do so was the most forgivable of his failures. Or it could've simply been his way of escaping the morning light – the curtains were long past threadbare. Yet in that burrowed twist, the sun had a habit of illuminating the sad dome of his bald spot with the most poignant of shines. How the light filled the place then. All glasses and bottles would be set aglint, with swathed halos of dust rising ghostly from the floorboards. These empty vessels of his night's work were everywhere, strewn in sorrow's endless complexity. If houses have auras, and I believe they do, then the aura of our little bungalow was never clearer than at that time of day.

The clouds of his bad dreams hung above us both throughout the waking hours. I left him to himself, which I suppose was his wish. It wasn't all bad, far from it. There was a tremendous freedom on offer. Wouldn't it have been a sin not to embrace that? Life had taken greatly from me, but it gifted something else. What seem like curses can be blessings. Then again, what seem like blessings can be fucking curses.

The days and nights were mine and I did with them as I pleased. The drinking, well, it was so different from the old fellow's it was hard to see the relation. The excitement of those early cans – the fervour they demanded, the illicit ritualism. Those early epic journeys to Murphy's: myself, Monk, Bubble Brady, and Nobby. The offie was on the edge of town, past the forest, past the lake. Starting at the football pitch, we'd leap walls and hedges, cut across fields. The lazy dirty stream of slagging flowing through us along the way as real as the landscape. Bubble sneering, shouldn't Nobby be getting back to the workshop? You know, before Santy notices. Elf-eared and bird-boned Nobby – puberty left his delicacy pretty much untouched. Then Nobby asking Bubble had his mother forgiven him. For the wreck he made of her fanny. That she must be a saint. That with that noggin of his, he must've had the poor woman stretched from here to Cork the day she bore him. Monk and his heaving haw of a donkey laugh cajoling them on. He was the size of each of us combined and escaped all but the most cursory of digs. I got off lightly too. The commonest go at me was about the daydream deep into which I'd often sink. Spacer, I was sometimes called. Yes, my mind had a drifting tendency, even then.

It was by the water we brought the cans most often. Around where Mammy used to take me as a little fellow to feed the swans. Every Sunday, just the two of us. The picture of it has turned clear again. The stories she told about them, too. Stories that were so easy to believe. For weren't they feathered leviathans from my infant vantage. Great beaks scary-sharp against my hands, nicking the skin along with the bread. But vulnerability, too, in their hungry pinches. Mammy saying they needed us as we needed them.

The drinking was done in a nook at the top. By the hill leading up to the forest entrance on the town side. Crags of rock our barstools, rustled music from the trees above. Whispers through the branches. The wind-allure of the forest. There were other spots – a go-nowhere boreen near the school, an old outhouse on Kirk's farm, a building site behind the marshes where the building never got going. But nothing beat the lake.

Especially on those never-ending summer evenings. And when it turned night, there was a boundlessness too in the dark. A boundlessness that seeped into the water and became part of it. The countryside vanished black. It could've been an ocean.

The girls would gather too. With their laughter. So much lighter and welcoming than ours. Their touch, which could fleece all thought. Their skin and scent. They brought complications, both good and bad. The cans made it easier to say and do things that otherwise would not be said or done. If it went well, you'd pair up and disappear up the hill. If not, you were stuck chatting to Nobby. Rarely went well for him, poor chap. Bubble would make a holy show of himself. Slagging the girls he liked even more than he did Nobby. But he did ok. It was Monk though who had most success. He might've had that shame of fresh-grown pimples, but he was looming and magnetic in the way we all wished to be. And he was playing midfield an age level up to boot. The carnal cache of such a feat was no small thing. The games the rest of us required were for him unnecessary. Sure I'd have to be fully tanked to say hello. Monk only had to mooch over and that'd be that. Even with Mairead Keogh. Ahh, Mairead, Mairead. With her fairytale hair. You could envision her daisy-sized and having japes with bees and birds. You know the type.

Mairead could make pure trolls of some. Not of Gráinne though. And it was Gráinne I most often made it with. Gráinne Tully. Of Tully Butchers, the main one in town. From when we were small, she worked there. Sweeping up, little jobs, before ending up behind the counter. Red-head pretty Gráinne. Developed for her age too. Of the earth. In the group, she was often flinty with us lads, hard as the ground. You'd do well to get a smile. No nonsense. The way those who start work young are. Alone with you, though, she brightened and could be as malleable as clay. And the filthy mouth on her. Yanking you off, she'd be talking about yanking as much as she was yanking. Talking to your mickey as well as to you. Didn't mind that at all. Has her way with meat, Bubble said, with a smile that smarmered on beyond the gag.

Behind the forest wall we'd go. Treading over bushes — wary not to fall arseways and get bramble-shredded. Couldn't see each other, such was the black. Only feel that messy press of flesh, blind hands busy under shirts and skirts. Bumbling rummages, then a groove. All sweet tension and electricity. Breaths, low groans. But these were not the only sounds. The whispers were loudest behind that wall. Yes, from around when we started drinking there, I heard them. Whispers from deep within the trees. Not so much words as airy enticements. Beckoning breezes.

'D'ya hear?' I asked once.

Her lips had left my lips and were journeying elsewhere.

'Hear what?' she said, stopping, getting flinty.

'Something in the forest.'

'A bit of wind just.'

'Sort of. But more like a voice. Like a voice that's more than a voice.'

'Only voice I hear is your croaking,' she said, doing up a button, then another. 'Never got what away with fairies was till I met you.'

It was the only occasion I mentioned them. Those wind whispers, their honeyed call. Every time I was there. And the more I drank, the louder they were.

My fate got sealed a night soon after. This fate was linked to my talent. Beware of them, your talents. Mine lay in my capacity. Not even Monk could best me. With him, there was a stopping point. His spot in midfield had to be considered. That imposed a limit. During the season, anyway. For me, there were no seasons, no such limits. All that held me back was the supply. I could throw it back all night long. One, two, three, to fuck knows how many. The lift you'd get, chucking them rapid. High as you could go. Manifolds surging through you. And then, not too long after, past that point. Past possibility. The possibilities disappeared. All together at once. Bang. Everything disappeared. Except for the slide. That sweet black slide. The rush of that too. Best rush of all, in fact. Oblivion. Especially in the dark, out in the open. Between the water and whispers from the trees. The space we shared turning to nothing – a dream.

It was the beginning of June. The exams had finished, we'd been celebrating. All things considered, I didn't do so dreadfully. But schooling wasn't to be in my present much longer. It was merely another excuse to gather if excuses were needed. That night, Monk had gone off with Mairead. Bubble had disappeared early and Gráinne hadn't shown up at all. She had to work early, she'd said. Lately, there'd been squabbles. All messy, all a blur. After a few, she could get prickly, to put it nicely. Yet it was my proclivity she took issue with. Plastered,

I was either stuck to her – 'plaster-stuck', she said – or else it was as if I didn't know her from Eve. Which version she disliked the more she couldn't say. The cheek! She was the fickly one. Nuzzling up all eyes and lips only when the mood took hold. Who the fuck did she think she was? And on it would go.

So it was just me and Nobby in the night's dregs. In the dark. By the water. Not saying much at all. Most of the little spoke was spoke by Nobby. About the past, our early schooldays. Evaporated time. Then, out of the dark, Nobby said he was sorry. He wanted to tell me again. About Mammy. It was roundabouts the anniversary of her passing – three or so years before. Trust Nobby to remember. At school, then at the graveside, the lads offered the same eyes-to-the-ground condolences. Whatever small words they could. He was the only one to hold my gaze then. You see, Nobby lost his mother, too. He'd barely hurdled infancy. It was a malignancy also.

The cancer took its while with Mammy. The fags, her demon. It started with the throat. Then ate her up piece by piece. All the time pretending things were fine. That she wasn't a walking skeleton. A skeleton cooking. A skeleton playing with her food. A skeleton struggling to even lift her beloved hardbacks. A coughing skeleton watching TV. And then a skeleton who couldn't get out of bed. A shrunken skeleton in the hospice. A buried skeleton. There, under the earth, staying even a skeleton was too hard. Easier to crumble. No choice really. It wasn't something I was inclined dwell upon. Especially stocious. I thanked Nobby, said I appreciated him saying so, and said no more.

The forest listened, as it stayed listening. Watching. Waiting. That night, the restless itch was undampened, however much

I drank. I didn't want to be with Nobby. I didn't want to be with anyone. I wanted to be out there among the trees. The wind-voice, it was calling. Louder than before. More and more, the booze was allowing me to tune into its register. It was old, very old, the voice. As old as the trees. That I could tell. Older maybe. I could hear it even after the first couple of cans. After a dozen, it was a whisper no longer. It was a siren call. A gorgeous wooing whistle. A siren-sweet whistling woo. Not just that – it was a promise of comfort unending. Nobby had turned to talking of his own mother, but it was almost all I could hear.

I told Nobby I had to go and took off across the road, up the hill. Past the entrance, into the forest. Down the main path, then off the path. With uncertain hands I went forward, edging further. Only guided by that voice.

How long I was at this I've no notion. All I wanted was to steep my senses away, let the enfolding darkness in. All of it. Gráinne had taken a shine to Bubble. That I knew. The sly glances she'd started flickering at that warped-headed bastard were enough to be sure. It was over between us. But that didn't really matter, not a jot. The urge lay deeper. I wanted to banish our bungalow and its dust. Daddy on the couch – that damnable couch would be his coffin. And Mammy. And Mammy. And Mammy most of all. I cursed Nobby to hell for bringing her up. Or maybe there was something else, something below and beyond even Mammy. Something beneath thought, something so deep there are no words for. On and on I lurched, every footfall an almost trip. Branches slapped and scraped me in spite of my care. You've no idea what woods are until you're in them after the sun goes down. Daylight masks their pagan hearts. But on and on and on I went. And the trees, in their grudging way, allowed me inside.

Eventually, I came to a clearing. As soon as I entered, the voice ceased. And as soon as I entered, I knew I wasn't alone. It was an impossibility to be certain, but at the clearing's centre was what appeared to be a man. Sitting on a tree stump or rock. Stooped as he was, and dark as it was, you could tell he was a tower of a figure. Because of the dark, he looked nothing less than an outgrowing of the forest itself. Some fucking tree-man, more tree than man. There I stood and there he sat. Not a trace of a whisper between us. Then, in an unearthly rumble, the tree-man banished the quiet with a tyrant's whim. God, the noises that sprung from him. Barely human. A great song of grunts and groans that'd palpitate the dead. I hoped to Christ I wasn't walking in on some want-to-be devil taking a dump. Or worse.

Next thing I was on my knees. The whole place had gone spinning awhirl. Like all the booze I'd ever drunk hit me in one go. Every drop together in a tidal crash. Whoosh. And in the eye of the gyre, I saw him rise. Towards me he sailed, groaning no more – the drum beat of his walking stick the only sound. There was something else in the other hand. A glimmering something that stung your sight clean.

Before I knew it, he was right there. A righteous hairy tower. The dizziness went dizzier, and dizzier still. He grounded the walking stick and whatever else he held. With freed hands he cupped my face, hoisting me upright. His face was long and gnarled, but his hands were as soft and unblemished as a child's. His beard looked as if it contained birds and tiny feral creatures long extinct. The air changed around him. It felt like rain was coming but the sky was clear.

The words poured out in a rushed hushed babble. His wind-breath smelled of all the seasons mingled into one – death and birth, the whole shebang. I couldn't make head nor tail of his blather. He was speaking what I took to be Irish, but it wasn't any Irish I knew. When he saw I didn't have a clue what he was on about he hissed and spun around. Why he needed a walking stick I don't know. He was light on his feet for the giant he was – he could've been a dancer. Springing low, he scooped the glimmering thing he laid down moments before. He spoke again, English this time. But the English was slow, mangled. He held outstretched a vessel. 'Drink' he boomed. Then slowly: 'Ól an deoch.'

It was a can. A golden can. A beer can, or something like it. Larger than the usual kind, though otherwise not very re-markable – its glimmer was fading. The silhouette of a black cauldron darkened its surface. It was no brand I recognised. The black of the cauldron was different from the black of the night, and the black of the forest. It was a black you could lose yourself in. I could tell even then.

The threat of rain passed and the darkness around us light-ened. He was younger than I thought; however, his eyes had an antediluvian innocence bruised by time. In that lightening dark, his irises performed sparkling pirouettes. Feeling a tad steadier, I took the can. 'Drink,' he boomed again. 'Ól.'

Any fear I had trickled away. I could say I struggled, spat in his face, told him to disappear right the fuck off. But if I told you this it'd be an epic lie. Somehow, I knew this was all I was after, what I came for. But I gave the opening a sniff to make sure he didn't piss in it, or anything. If it was his piss, it smelled divine. Downed it in one go, ahhh. Only then did he shut up. Fuck, that first taste! Nothing before came close. It was like beer but wasn't. Not wine either. Somewhere between the two. Or a blend. Honeyed, whatever it was. Not just tinged but suffused with the stuff. Succulent. Strong and smooth-sweet. So, so sweet. Not the sickly kind. Not at all. An invigorating sweetness. The kick it gave. Life-giving. Bounteous. What mattered most of all was I wanted more. God, how I wanted more. But it was gone.

He laughed in mania, not mirth. Out of that laugh leapt the chasmed echo of loss. Just when I was about to throw the can away, I stopped. For it felt liquid-heavy – the weight had somehow returned. He started once more with his talk: 'Drink up, drink up, you will never drink your fill.' He motioned me to drink. The can was full. Jesus, I must've been more pissed than I'd thought. I downed it again. And again the same thing happened. The can never emptied. Or rather, once empty, it became full.

As much as he laughed, he seemed always on the verge of wailing. Then I sat down, and he talked. If he didn't think I was paying due attention he'd stick his tongue out and do that hiss of his, so I tried my very best to listen. My memory of what he said is sketchy, though, and comes mainly from the dreams I've had about that night since. The crux of it was the can was mine if I wished it to be. All the booze I could drink for life. To others the can would appear a regular can. Its magic was for me alone. I drank and he talked, and I drank and he stayed talking. He could talk for Ireland. The more he went on, the more mellifluent he became. His English needed space and time to unfurl. But it's the sound, that deep windful boom of his, I remember most. And how it all appeared natural and right that I was there with him that night, in that clearing. That it was the only way things could be.

By morning, he was gone. I awoke cradling the can as a child does his toy. It was full again, of course. Not only that, the seal had closed. The night was no dream. My head, Lord, it was throbbing. The pillow of a tree root I'd laid on hadn't done the hangover any favours. But how I laughed and laughed at the savage wonder of it all. I laughed how that stupid Midas cunt must've done when granted the golden touch. I got up, dusted myself, clicked it open and had another wee sup. Fuck it was tasty, almost as good as before. I couldn't help but scull it there, among the trees, under the morning sun that promised so much. In my hand, I felt its magic brewing and bubbling as it grew heavier again, its lusciousness replenishing. You could imagine it keeping going, rising and rising until it spilled forth in great geyser torrents. Drowning the trees, the forest, and flowing down to the lake. And keeping going still, turning the lake into an ocean, an ocean of booze, flooding the town in giant frothy sticky waves of piss-gold. The county, the country after that, lost in the can-deluge, until our little island was wiped from the map. Good riddance. That didn't happen, needless to say. The brew stopped when it reached the top like before. It was for me alone, as he'd said. The voice of the tree-man, I heard that too. It came not from the forest but from within. *Would you not have another?* it said. *Look at what a lovely day it is. Sure what else would you be doing?* So that is what I did. I made my way down, down to our spot by the lake, and had myself another and another and then another.

And so it was the following day and the one which followed. The next few weeks, months – even years – had a not dissimilar flavour to what came before. After that, well, I could tell you how the can made working tricky, and relationships trickier. Until all was a tangle. A desperate fucking tangle. Sometimes the tangle needed cutting, by me or by others. More often than not, the knots loosened, as if by themselves. Time lending its hand. A skilled loosener is time. The can helped too, feigning to forget it made the bloody tangle in the first place. Then a point was reached when there was nothing left. Nothing except the can.

Never tasted as sweet as it did in those early days. Yet through all the regular lows, and the depths beyond, it's left my side only rarely. Have I tried ridding myself of the damned thing? Of course I have! In the midst of the most wrathful storms, I've thrown it into the Atlantic from precipices steep. Buried it in bogs. Watched it burn in fires that turned all else to dust. Chucked it into bins. Lots of bins. Lots and lots. No bloody difference. The result is always the same. Every morning I awake and there it is. Full to the brim. With its dark sparkle. The untarnished gold, the black of the cauldron. The seal closed like it was off the shelf. And every morning I take a swig whether I want to or not. The matter of choice gone with the tree-man, with the years.

Every damnable day I come here. Have a sup, then another. The time, it goes up in smoke. A grey or yellow haze, depending on the light. Then night's emptiness, the same dreams of the forest. The trees, they are a comfort, yes. But when the dark comes, I see the shadow of his face in them. His eyes. And in the laughing groups by the water, there's the shadow of our own little tribe. My knowledge of their fates is patchy. Monk got his championships. That I know. A midfield bulldozer with a touch that belied his size. Carried the team on his back the story goes. Bubble and Gráinne, they ended up wed. Took over Tully's, the two of them. Bubble The Butcher. It has a ring. As for Nobby, ah, he never had the best of luck. Suffered a bad crash. Many moons ago now. The blackest of the local blackspots, not far from Murphy's. Pretty tanked by all accounts. Would've liked to have made the funeral. But I was in London and not in the best shape. Not in the best shape at all.

When I join Nobby, Daddy, Mammy, and the rest of them underground, the can will be all that remains. The tree-man will return for it, you can be sure. That's what the dreams say. And he'll pass it to another, like he passed it to me. Like he passed it to countless others, just like those in the laughing gangs. Their gangs will not keep them safe. It'll be passed to the one with the greatest thirst. To the one that remains when the rest have gone homeward. To the one who doesn't want to go home. The one who has no home. *Have a drink*, the tree-man will say. *Just a little sup. What harm will it do?* Fuck them and their laughter. They think youth will keep them floating. One day they'll drown and think they're swimming. Think they're swimming for gold as they drown the same drown of their forebears. Ah, the poor fuckers.

I stay until there's no one left. It's just me and the can. Have a sup, then another. The swan too. Later than usual, but she came. Clear, even in this dark. A miracle of white. The white a child imagines heaven to be. The little laps she makes drifting on the still water, ever so gentle. The city sounds fall away.

When she is here, the ill will fades. *Let go*, she says. *Look at the trees, the water. Look at them and let go*. Ah, yes. She has come to me, to me alone. I'd the spirit of a hunch. But only now do I fully realise. It is too late, though. Too late by a distance. If only I'd a crumb or two for her. I only have the can. But she does not care. Look at her approach. The mammoth wings extending – ahh, what a sight and sound. With royal flurry she ascends. And in a bell-beat, she is there beside me. Close-up the dazzle is almost too much to take. Almost frightening. *Avert your eyes*, she says. Stoops her neck, nestling in.

I put the can on the bench's arm and reach down. There, there. Stroke her as she tells me to do. My hand buries deep. God what softness. God-cloud softness. I fear I've gone too far. What right have I to touch so brilliant a creature? But she says, *No, it's all right. It's ok. Rest. Take your time. Time means little to me*. She'll fly off to join her kind, in some other world, but not for a while. So I bury myself deeper in the warmth and comfort of her. Once I yearned to forget, but now I crave the opposite. My eyes, they close. And I dream. Dreams different to the dreams of the tree-man in the clearing. Dreams I've not had for years. Momentary dreams that haven't a chance of transpiring. Yet I cling to them regardless. I cling to them because I've nothing else. And try to be grateful for that small mercy.

My eyes stay closed. I cannot bear to see her go. Time washes away and then, a gigantic clamour. The air whirls. The bell-beat of those wings, how mighty they are. Roaring thunders of mythic motion. Up they go, further and further. They fill the sky. I hear them, hearing nothing else. I hear them until I hear nothing. And I turn to the bench's arm to see what's there.

MÁIRE T. ROBINSON

ENSNARED

They say that the sweetest sound to someone's ear is their own name, but when I meet these men on dates, I hear mine as a mangled thing; an unexpected pip in a soft, sweet fruit, a lump of a thing to be tongued with confusion, then spat out. So, when we meet and he kisses me on both cheeks and calls me by the wrong name, I don't correct him. I smile.

I was sitting on the sofa at home doing the sip-and-scroll when I first saw his profile. It's how I spend most of my evenings: sipping pinot grigio and scrolling dating apps.

Sip, sip… swipe left.

Sip, sip… swipe right.

I like my wine cold. Keep a wine glass in the fridge. Even put white grapes in the freezer and use them as ice cubes. Still, it is somehow never cold enough.

The profiles start to look the same after a while, as though there is some sort of secret manual men are using to fill out these things. His included the standard photo of him with a small child. A grin to say: "Check it out, ladies! See how good I am with kids. Doesn't it just make your ovaries tingle?" But a caption to reassure them: "The baby is my niece!"

My date looks better than in his photos. Sitting opposite him, he is almost unnaturally beautiful. I can feel the eyes of everyone in the room on him, but he is looking only at me. At the bar they are offering Halloween-themed cocktails. We read the names from the drinks menu: Zombie, Vampire's Kiss, Piña Ghoulada…

'Green Fairy?' he says. 'That's not very Halloween-y.'

'Why not?'

'Well, they're hardly very scary, are they?'

I correct him. 'Faeries are terrifying.'

He laughs as though I have made a tremendous joke. He's probably picturing tiny winged things flitting about the place like in cartoons, but I'm remembering Granny's stories of *Daoine Maithe*.

'They're cunning,' I tell him. 'And they can look like regular people. That's how they trick you and trap you in their world forever. You might not even realise before it's too late.'

He holds his hands up, palms facing outward as though in supplication.

'Okay, okay. Well, I don't go in for any of that.'

I'm not sure if he means faeries or faffy drinks. Maybe both. We agree to forgo the cocktails and stick with our usuals. He goes to the bar and I study him surreptitiously while pretending to look at the Bar Bites menu.

'So, Sarah, how was your day?'

He is back and placing a glass of white wine in front of me. Now is the time to tell him he's gotten my name wrong but I can't seem to do it. It probably doesn't matter anyway. This date will go like the others and I won't see him again after tonight. Besides, being Saoirse has gotten me nowhere and I like the shape of his mouth as he says Sarah.

'Oh, not too bad, thanks. I was at the dentist. Got a filling.'

Earlier, when I was waiting to be called into the dentist's room, I ran my tongue over my broken filling as I flipped through magazines, the kind I never buy for myself. I stopped on an article about "snaring" a man. I rolled my eyes but kept reading. Snare — like capturing some flighty thing. A nervous bird or a small woodland animal. Something that does not belong to you. The trick, according to this magazine, was to make him think he was the one chasing you. I probed the jagged edge of my tooth again. It hurt but I had this compulsion to keep doing it. I wondered if I'd miss the sensation once the tooth was fixed.

The dentist told me he needed to take an x-ray. I assured him I wasn't pregnant, resisted the urge to make a joke about the immaculate conception as he turned and started to prepare the shiny, metal implements he would put inside my mouth.

I've been waiting for that certainty I've heard I should be experiencing at my age – that biological impulse telling me that I need to have children and have them now. But it hasn't arrived. All I feel is a vague sense of days passing, time slipping by, options becoming narrower. Sometimes I hear myself speaking again in that hypothetical way about some future imaginary offspring, saying 'Some day, if I have children…' but it's in that same way I've mentioned over the years, with an ever-decreasing lack of enthusiasm, the possibility of visiting Africa – 'Oh, I'd love to go there at some point!' Meanwhile, I am still here and Africa is still there: an entire continent oblivious of me, alone on my own small island.

Reclining in the dentist's chair, I opened my jaw as wide as I could. Felt a latexed finger in my mouth. There was something erotically charged about it, even though when I looked up all I could see was half the dentist's masked face. I gripped the arm rests and looked at the ceiling. Was it the giving over of power, the vulnerability, the fear of physical damage? If the drill should slip. Pierce the soft flesh of the inside of my mouth. That tightrope wire of possible injury. I stared past him to the ceiling-mounted TV screen instead. A rolling banner of news headlines. Bizarre weather forecasted. Red dust over Dublin City on the way, blown in from the Sahara.

My date leans in closer. 'Not too painful, I hope?'

I look at him blankly.

He smiles. 'The dentist?'

'Oh! No, no, it was fine,' I reassure him.

Absently, I run my tongue over the tooth. When I sip my drink, the glass is warm like it's not long out of the dishwasher. Suddenly, I feel tired and it all seems pointless and I wish I was at home by myself. Sipping and scrolling. Scrolling and sipping. The beautiful lull of it. The real-life meetings are never as satisfying as the small worlds contained on the phone screen. But no, my date is smiling at me, and leaning forward doing that intent listening thing. I tell myself I'm not being fair. I smile back. I ask him a question about his job and then instantly regret it because he starts telling me, actually telling me, about it. Other people's jobs are incomprehensible most of the time. A series of languages I recognise a few key phrases in but lack the fluency to fully comprehend.

Why am I even here? These first dates never turn into second ones. Sasha, Sara, Sheena, Sheila waits for a follow-up message that never arrives. So, why do I keep doing this to myself? Well, I suppose it's that I got to thinking it would be nice to wake up with someone's arm around me. Cook breakfast together, read the Sunday papers. All that stuff. When I picture this scene, no particular person materialises. A faceless man, a tall man with good arms. It isn't so much sex I crave, but the things you can't replicate by yourself. The creeping need that porn and a vibrator can't satiate. The hulk and certainty of flesh, the weight of a man on top of me. Sweat. Spit. Cum. And other things too. You know that feeling when maybe you're just standing at the sink or something, not paying attention, and he comes up behind you and wraps his arms around your waist and kisses your neck and holds you just like that, and for that moment time stops? I haven't felt that for the longest time, but I remember. My body remembers.

Now they're calling last orders at the bar. My date has ordered chicken wings. He nibbles and slurps, probing them with an eager tongue. He sucks gristle.

'Help yourself,' he offers. He talks with his mouth full of bones.

The magazine article about snaring a man said to find things in common.

'Oh, no thanks. I do like wings though. I'm just not hungry at the moment. Don't worry, I'm not a vegetarian or anything.'

I don't elaborate further. But the thing is, I used to be vegetarian, for a time. I spent several years where eating meat was unthinkable, impossible. Flesh and blood, like me. But somehow, I had started to eat it again. Kept those old thoughts at a distance. Ignored the signals to my brain that meat was to be avoided. In time, I even began to enjoy the aroma, the taste. And I learned that you can condition yourself to feel nothing if you just stop thinking about it. My date smiles at me and I can see a sliver of flesh between his white teeth. I tongue my new filling. The spot feels warmer than the other teeth.

'So, Sarah, do you fancy coming back to my place for a nightcap?'

Saoirse has had a lot of nights like this that never lead to a second date, but things might work out differently for Sarah. I smile and put on my coat.

In the taxi, I wonder if this is it. How it will happen for me. Two people meet in a pub one night and end up creating a life together. Partners. Him getting my name wrong will be an amusing anecdote he'll share in his speech on our wedding day. Maybe we'll start going to garden centres at weekends, buying patio furniture, procreating. If we have children, we'll always have something to talk about. We can bring them to the park. Buy some photo frames. Remove the default paper-family photographs and replace them with our own smiling faces.

Back at his place, my date takes a packet of rashers and sausages wrapped in cling film from his freezer and leaves them to defrost on the kitchen counter. He says he will make me breakfast in the morning.

In bed, he puts his head between my legs. I feel his tongue search for my clit.

Three desultory licks.

Swipe. Swipe. Swipe.

Then his head appears from under the duvet like a hermit crab peeking from its shell. I smile down at his uncertain face and he takes this as a sign that he has done enough. He emerges triumphant, wiping his mouth with the back of his hand.

He fumbles with the condom wrapper for what feels like an eternity, rejecting my offer of help. Finally, I climb on top.

'Oh yes, Sarah,' he moans. 'Sar-AH!'

I close my eyes, picture my faceless man with good arms.

Afterwards I turn on my side. He wraps his arms around me and holds me so tightly that it's hard to breathe.

'I feel so close to you,' he murmurs into my hair. 'It's like we're an old married couple.'

And suddenly that is exactly what we are and I feel the age in my ancient bones like all of our days are already lived and gone, and there is only looking back now, not forward.

In his half-sleep he starts to talk about buying the newspaper and making me breakfast tomorrow. And I realise that he has a blank-faced woman of his own. And now the empty space is filling in with my features. One of Granny's old faerie stories flashes through my mind. A lost cailín who strays into an enchanted forest. She has long heard the warnings not to eat faerie food or drink faerie drink lest she be trapped in their world forever. *Don't let a morsel pass your lips… don't let a morsel pass your lips… don't let…* But she sees the most exquisite banquet laid out, too delicious to resist, and she is so very tired and so very hungry. Just a small bite. What harm? A warning unheeded. I think about that clump of meat defrosting. Becoming sinewy, giving up its hardness, its protective freeze, particles of ice dissolving.

If I am still here in the morning, by the time it has defrosted, I will never be able to leave. I know this now, feel it in my bones. It never occurred to me that a snare could be a warm bed, a place of comfort. How much easier to sink into this, not to fight. Was this his plan all along? How cheerily I marched into his trap. I rack my brain for stories of how to outwit faeries. Tales of familiar locales – a field, a boreen – becoming unpassable. Canny folk knowing the trick of turning coats inside-out to fool the Daoine Maithe and escape. But I'm not wearing a coat. Would I need to turn myself inside-out?

He starts to snore. I need to leave now without waking him, the only way to break this spell. I try to get up but his leg is resting on top of mine, anchoring me to the bed. It is unnaturally heavy. I try to move it, but it won't budge. He can't know that I am trying to escape. He will stop me. This parallel me will be trapped here forever with him. A kind of death.

I angle my upper body to reach my leg. Move my mouth to the edge of my thigh. Sink my teeth in above the knee. I bite through skin, muscle, sinew. Blood seeps warm, turns cold. Teeth strike bone. For a moment, I feel woozy, like I might pass out with the job half done, but I keep biting. All instinct, all adrenaline.

Must keep going. He stirs and I fear he is about to wake. I stop. Hold my breath…

Start again.

Nearly. Nearly. Nearly…

With a snap I'm free.

If I had both legs, I would tiptoe out. I crouch, half-hop, half-crawl to the front door. Grab my coat and wrap it around me. Pull up my hood. My mouth is metallic with the taste of my own blood. I don't stop, don't look back. I'm lighter, dizzy, euphoric.

The world outside looks new, cloaked in red dust. A fine layer coats car bonnets, window ledges, even the leaves of trees… And I am alone in this new redness. Until I am not.

I feel myself being watched. A snout. Twitching ears. One of those city foxes, I think. But no, look again. It is a wolf. The red dust giving its pale-grey coat a red sheen. We observe each other in silence.

I hear my name. At first, I think it is the wolf who speaks it. But no, the wolf remains silent. It is not the leaves whispering it. It is not carried in the skirl of dust that dances in circles on the pavement. Perhaps what I'm hearing is the blood pulsing inside my own head. And yet, it sounds like the atmosphere itself reverberating my name over and over in a low hum. Saoirse Saoirse Saoirse… The wolf turns and is gone. Into the redness.

Checking my teeth, I half expect to feel the rough edge of my new filling unloosed, but it is still there, smooth and solid against my tongue.

BLAISE GILBURD

DEATH OF A BEACHCOMBER

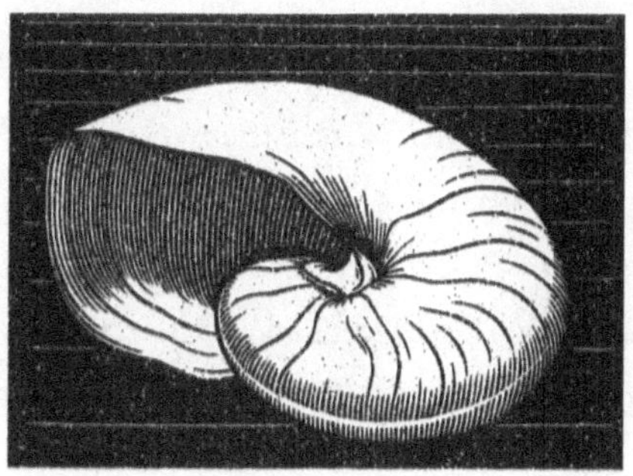

The sea slips up the beach and tickles the space between her toes before hissing back out over the shells and stones. She bends down, picks up a razor clam and rubs the sand off with her thumb. The end is chipped and she throws it out to sea. She walks a little further along, her eyes scanning over the emptied pockets of the tide. The rocks clock together as they roll backwards with the retreat of the waves. She squeezes the sand between her toes as the water runs over her feet. It is cold when the sun goes in, the wind that pulls her hair across her face carries the clear chill of the approaching winter. The water is icy but her feet have long since grown numb to it. She holds a plastic bag in one hand, hanging down by her side and flapping, and the other is free to pick up and inspect anything she finds.

A delicate orange periwinkle rolls in front of her toe; she takes it, holds it up in the light and squints at it. The tip is sharp and she can make out the lines that travel around and around to its point. The colour looks wonderful and vibrant, but it is always once they dry out you see the matter's truth. She holds it to her lips and blows any water or sand out of the chamber and deposits it in her bag. It is fitting, she thinks, once the shells are removed from the water they lose their lustre like dead coral and are never as beautiful as when they were in the sea. She wishes that she could just watch them in their wet vitality, their natural place, when their colours are most saturated.

Her sister had not so very long ago given birth to a happy and healthy daughter. She had been on the phone with her just before leaving the house. Afterwards, she wrapped herself in a thick parka and wandered down to the beach. She wants to make something for the baby. She looks again at the photo in the family WhatsApp group of the child's unbelievably tiny face. A mobile, she thinks, would be lovely, hanging above the baby's head, decorated with the treasures that she has collected from the beach and moving like the spin of the currents.

She sees a well-shaped mussel, a deep, dark blue sitting in the sand, and picks it up. They are the shape of bee's wings, and act as great spoons to slurp up sauce that they have been cooked in. She scoops some sand with it as she lifts it up before tipping the shell and letting it spill out. She does like the French style of cooking them: white wine, garlic and thyme, but her partner makes an amazing *merkén* mussel broth. So rich with chilli and spice! And when she is done, she has a whole bowl of beautiful shells the colour of a winter sea clacking together as she rinses them. She places the mussel in her bag and plucks a couple more from the sand around it.

The clouds are moving fast in the sky, chugging along in narrow bands and making it cold whenever they pass in front of the sun. Her ears ache a little from the rush of the wind over them, but the beach is all a roar. She cannot discern the waves crashing further out from shore from wind howling into her head. The waves look black when they rise up – that is how you know it is winter. Black and lipped with a thin crest of white foam. When they break, they slam into the water below and send volumes rushing to the seabed. Then the hiss and rush of white-water and foam kisses her feet delicately. It brings her treasures and leaves them for her to find, and the moon talks to the tide. It connects, behind the tarmac clouds, with the merciless blackness of the water. All spinning and motion that to stare into is to find yourself falling through space. You, in your core and heart, are tugged up and slung up towards the moon, pulled by that same force which dictates the way in which the water shall swallow the Earth.

What she wants to find peeking from the sand is some sea glass. The rounded little stones of foggy brown or green, smoothed by the rolling wash of the ocean's currents. She loves the implied history of a piece of glass, even more so one lost at sea that has been softened. Glass is sharp, dangerous like a blade and in the seeing and being seen. Yet these pieces have been sanded into something else. Who knows where a single piece could have come from or could have been? The stained glass window of a church sacked by Vikings or a bottle of beer thrown overboard by a drunkard out deep-sea fishing. Of all humanity's substances, it grows the most beautiful in our absence, but still links itself back to us. They really are like jewels and, to her, a treasure.

A scallop shell, she thinks, would be a good find too. Another shell in a shade of orange, more fleshy in colour, spread like a fan for fish. All the ones that she picked up have been shards or the pieces from which the shards came. They look complete when they sit half buried in the sand, but every time she pulls one out to inspect, it is never whole. Her partner makes a nice dish with scallops. It is arranged like a queen in checkers. They stack a piece of chorizo on a scallop, which is then stacked on some black pudding. The subtle sweetness of the black pudding and scallop mix well, the richness of the chorizo oil dripping down onto the shellfish.

She looks out at the waves against the horizon, violent and pummelling. They do not peel calmly like the glassy lefts of California. These waves are frothing and rabid and dump their contents like a heavy blow. She rolls up the cuffs of her trouser legs and the sudden exposure of skin gives her goosebumps. The wind catches the droplets splashed up when the water meets her leg and sprays them further up. She steps out a little further, up to her calves. They start throbbing. The water is cold.

Another wave breaks, slams down with a crash, and she notices something bobbing in the foamy entrails. The after-rush skimming across the surface carries the object closer to her; she can see that it is round and white. She rolls her trousers further up her leg until they are squeezing her thighs and wades out towards it.

The white thing in the foam is bobbing near to her. She cannot go any further out or she will soak her trousers and she can feel the chill of the water seeping into her lungs. It floats backwards a little bit before another slip of white-water pushes it back towards her. She stretches out one arm and extends it as far as she can, reaching for the object while trying not to lose her place and fall into the undulating surroundings.

The thing is pulled away from her by the water rushing back out to sea before again being pushed closer by the waves. This time she presses her fingers onto its surface and pulls it closer little by little. It is hard, but not as smooth as it looked, now it is all shiny and wet. When she has it close by her hip, she clasps the top of it with her hand, her fingers spread around the circumference, and begins to wade back to shore.

When the depth drops, she lifts the object from the water by its crown; water spills from the sockets and a hole in the base and she locks eyes with the skull. The colour looks like the inside of a limpet. Soft and white, but when you look at it more closely you see that the colour is more creamy, and you see the variations in pattern that you missed before. In fact, as the water runs off and it becomes drier and drier, like the shells it grows darker and less pristine. She walks out of the water and up to drier sand. Droplets tickle as they slide down her leg and she rubs them down and unrolls her trousers. The cold still lingers in her muscles. She places the skull down, its jaw sinking a little in the sand. She steps back and observes the skull with her hands on her hips. She considers it making the perfect centrepiece for her niece's mobile. She decides that the skull is a woman's, and notices that the gaze is fixated out at sea in the roar and the wash. She wonders what the skull is looking at and turns around, feeling sharp flecks of sand scratch her face. There is foam and the island black against the sky. She sits beside the skull and buries her hands and feet in the sand as she stares at the ocean.

'What is it?' she asks. 'What are you looking for?'

The skull stares. She notices something rolling up the beach as the tidal suck draws the water out. From where she sits it looks like a branch, some driftwood bleached by years at sea. There was a morning a few years back, following one of the worst storms they had seen in years, when her, her partner and the dog came across a whole tree while walking the beach. Tossed across the ocean from somewhere else and deposited like it was nothing more than a stray branch in a stream. She stands up and the wind is pulling at her again and the waves whisper from the shoreline for her to come. The object still rolls as she walks quickly down to the water, picks the humerus up from the sand and brushes it off. It is startlingly light. She waves with it to the skull watching her from the dunes.

The skull continues to be silent as she stumbles in the sand up to it and lays the bone down in the sand in front of her.

'Look,' she says, smiling, 'it was in the water.'

The skull continues to watch the waves, so she turns and sees more white objects rolling in the shallows up and down the beach.

There are two hundred and six bones in the human body, she had once read somewhere. Or had her partner told her that? Either way, there were nowhere near that many assembled before her now, with the skull at the top. Just enough were laid out to give the outline of a body, like an exhibit in a museum.

The bones had been scattered the length of the beach, from the base of the cliffs where waves whirled in a foam to the stretch of rocks and boulders that extended out to sea. She had left her bag of shells with the skull and ran back and forth collecting bones as they rolled in with the tide. When her arms were full, she would run up to the skull as if carrying a pile of tinder and drop them in the sand with a rattle. She spent almost an hour doing this relay, watching the water and sprinting from piece to piece and back up the beach until she was bent double in the shallows, her hands on her knees and panting. When it was just little toe bones rolling in, metatarsals and phalanges, she gave up.

It has formed a skeleton around the skull, not that the presence feels so very different. The tide has crawled up the beach whilst she was retrieving the bones and now waits only a few metres away from where she sits.

'You know, I'm not sure the day or time,' she says, 'but I'm glad I am able to spend it with you.'

The skeleton continues to stay silent as sand blows through its rib cage and sifts down the beach.

'I am so excited to meet my niece,' she says.

She looks at the bones, at the little black specks of beach hoppers springing about within the hollows and empty spaces. They hop at her and make her arm itchy, so she buries them under sand. She remembers being buried. The water inches closer as she lifts the skull from the rest of the body and places it on her lap, and together they watch the black clouds roll out of the breach in the horizon. She can see the swathes of grey rain heaving in the sky, dark pillars descending. All these things approach, the rain and the tide and she thinks about where her partner might be, whether the dog misses her, whether the dog remembers her?

The cold of the water and the cut of the wind. When she looks down again the water is at her feet. She jumps up, drops the skull and looks at the skeleton.

'Get up,' she shouts, 'get up, the tide is here!'

She steps back and squeezes her arms into her chest.

'Please move, the water is almost on you,' she says.

The skeleton lies prone and the water writhes up through the bones, gasping and sucking. She steps back again in a rush as her feet are almost swallowed by the tide. The bones are picked up from the sand and pushed towards her, and as the water begins to peel back the skull rolls and the bones are bobbing out to sea again and she can see the skull as only a white thing floating in the black water. She starts to cry, sat amongst the hissing grasses in the dunes. Why must things change?

She waits for the tide to change course. When it does eventually begin to run away from her she feels it drawing the heat from her body and sucking it into the open ocean. Before the tide has receded entirely she thinks for a moment about how much she would have liked to have met her niece, and then returns to combing the beach for the remnants of dead things deposited by the sea.

The sea slips up the beach and tickles the space between her toes before hissing back out over the shells and stones. She bends down, picks up a razor clam and rubs the sand off with her thumb.

THE AUTHORS

A mass of tentacles and rose vines masquerading as a person, AMANDA M. BLAKE is the author of such horror titles as *Question Not My Salt*, *Deep Down*, and *Out of Curiosity and Hunger*, the dark poetry collection *Dead Ends*, and the *Thorns* fairy tale mash-up series. For more, visit amandamblake.com

KIT CALVERT (**she/her**) is a Scottish speculative fiction writer and scientist, currently based in Edinburgh. Her work weaves together nature that's wild and weird, domestic magics, and unapologetic queer joy. When she's not writing, she enjoys foraging for treasures in rockpools, painting, and consuming an irresponsible amount of soup.

COREY FARRENKOPF lives on Cape Cod and works as a librarian. His work has been published in *Electric Literature*, *The Southwest Review*, *Nightmare*, *The Deadlands*, *SmokeLong Quarterly*, *Catapult*, and elsewhere. He is the author of the novel *Living in Cemeteries*, and the short story collection *Haunted Ecologies*. To learn more, visit his website at CoreyFarrenkopf.com

BLAISE GILBURD is an Irish writer raised in Galway and has just finished his MA in Literature and Publishing there. His work has previously appeared in *The Martello*, *Tír na nÓg*, *Skylight47*, *Crossways* and *Here Comes Everyone*. In 2019, he was awarded the NUIG Creative Arts Performance Points Scholarship.

ÉADIE LONG is an Irish creative based in Dublin. While not working on their day job as a game designer, they enjoy writing stories, making music, and exploring new places.

FRÉDÉRIC MATHIEU is a German-Irish writer of prose fiction, poetry, plays, essays, and screenplays. His television screenplay received an AMF Development Grant and was optioned by Causeway Pictures. His work was included in the Arvon Foundation's anthology *Casting Shadows*. He recently completed a Creative Writing MPhil at Trinity College Dublin.

ROSS MCCLEARY is from Edinburgh. His work has appeared in *Structo*, *Litro*, *Baltimore Review*, and *Extra Teeth*. He believes in repetition and Carly Rae Jepsen.

AMY LYNNE MCKENZIE's work has appeared in *Kenyon Review* and *American Short Fiction*. She lives with her partner and two feisty pets on an island in the Puget Sound, where she's always on the hunt for a good ghost story.

PAUL MULHOLLAND is a writer and editor based in Blackrock, Co. Louth.

DANIELLE MULLEN's work can be found in print and online. She's proud to have a piece in the anthology *Soul Jar: Thirty One Fantastical Tales From Disabled Authors* from Forest Avenue Press, which has been named a 2024 Top Ten science fiction/fantasy/horror book by Booklist. She lives, knits, and writes in Southern New Mexico.

AISLING NÍ CHOIBHEANAIGH NIC EOIN is a bilingual writer and creator from Galway. She was accepted onto the 2023 National Mentoring Programme with the IWC, and one of her poems was recently published by Blueway Art Studio in their hand-printed *Book for Brigid*. She is the co-founder and editor of the multilingual literary journal *Aimsir*.

ANNA NÍ DHÚILL is a theatre-maker and writer from Kilkenny. Their practice encompasses writing, directing and producing theatre and film projects that explore universal feeling, with a distinct focus on queer identity and expressionism.

MÁIRE T. ROBINSON is the author of the novel *Skin Paper Stone* (2015). More recent work includes short fiction in *Southword*, *Ropes*, and *The Waxed Lemon*; and creative nonfiction in *Banshee*, *Trasna*, and on *Sunday Miscellany*.

SCOTTY SARAFIAN is a Florida-born writer who grew up in Dublin, Ireland, and Wilmington, Delaware. He was shortlisted for Ghost Orchid Press's *A Very Ghostly Christmas* flash fiction contest and published in the accompanying anthology. He was also longlisted for Pulp Literature's 2023 Raven Short Story Contest. His work has appeared in publications and anthologies from Black Hare Press, Neon Hemlock (*Opulent Syntax: Irish Speculative Fiction*), Skywatcher Press (*The Depths Unleashed: Book 1*), Horror Tree (*Trembling with Fear*), among others. He lives in Dublin.

NORA SCHINNERL (she/her) lives in a shared house on the outskirts of Vienna, Austria, and tries not to get confused by writing in English while speaking in German. Her short fiction has previously appeared in *Future SF Digest*, *Escape Pod* and *Best of World Science Fiction Vol. 3*.

Sans.
PRESS

LIMERICK

2025

www.ingramcontent.com/pod-product-compliance
Lightning Source LLC
Chambersburg PA
CBHW031958180726
48283CB00008B/2486